RUTHLESS PROTECTOR

A FLOSSIN' ON STILETTO WHEELS DUET

MELVERNA MCFARLANE

MCFARLANE PUBLISHING LLC

AUTHOR'S NOTE

I had a lot of fun with Lucien and Zaïre and I hope you
will too.
P.S. There's a lot of sex.

SENSITIVE TOPICS

In Ruthless Protector, you will find the following topics.

- Violence
- Murder
- Torture
- Graphic Sex Scenes (Did I mention there's a lot of them?)
- Kidnapping

Please keep your mental health in mind if you find these topics distressing or triggering.

KEEP UP WITH MELVERNA MCFARLANE

Join Melverna McFarlane's newsletter to get updates, bonus scenes, and more. For a Lucien and Zaïre have a bonus scene as well. Check it out by signing up for my newsletter.

DEDICATION

Ruthless Protector is my ninth published story. The only way I've been able to keep the stories coming is because of the support you've given me. Thank you so much for being such dedicated readers and supporters of my work. Now, don't mind me as I dive into another story coming out soon.

CHAPTER ONE

Zaïre

*F*elicidad might as well be a world away from my little corner of heaven. Although a Floridian metropolis with a unique flair, nothing beats my beloved New Orleans, and I can't wait to return.

By all rights, my sister, Camille, should have made this trip to woo Mr. Gio "Don't Call Me Giorgio" Oliveri. His reputation for badassery is well known and one we want to ally ourselves with.

Of my three Roudanez sisters, Camille is the oldest. She is the firstborn and our best negotiator. If not for her, I wouldn't have joined—translation: been roped into co-founding—our club, Flossin' on Stiletto wHeels, a sister club to our daddy's Bayou Hellraisers.

So, why am I here even though approaching the Oliveris was Camille's idea? Because I lost a bet.

On any old regular day, I know better than to bet on a

race with Camille. Her first language isn't English. It ain't even our granddaddy's Kouri-Vini. No, her first language is motorcycle. All she has to do is look at one to know how fast it and the rider can go. Me, Zaïre Roudanez, second daughter to Émile, aka Hammer, Roudanez, with a master's degree in finance and a business owner at thirty-two? I'm not that intuitive. When I get near a bike, I care more about how it feels between my thighs as I take it on the road. But she'd riled me up in the way sisters do. And seeing as how I'm in a taxi on my way to check into my hotel instead of on my Hayabusa driving on the I-10, Camille's ulterior motive begins to dawn on me.

Rides to South Florida are best with the whole gang and require a lot of logistical planning to ensure our safety on the road. With the stress of maintaining the Flossers' reputation, growing our foothold, and protecting what's ours, there weren't enough members to ride. Therefore, a trip to Felicidad meant a flight. Given a choice, Camille would never set foot on a plane. And since she is our First Lady, she has many choices, including the choice of delegation. As second-in-command, my only way out was to accept a bet I had no way of winning.

Damp heat hits me the moment I step out of the taxi. It's soon countered by the cool air conditioning in the hotel lobby. My heels click on the cool marble floors of this modern, boutique hotel and I pass cold glass and steel to the front desk. Like the ride from the airport, everything in this city has a newborn feel, even the luxury surrounding me. There's no history. No music. And not enough seasoning in the air to put me completely at ease.

The first thing I do as I enter my suite is kick off my four-inch heels, sink my feet into the plush carpeting, and open my suitcase. My phone rings the second my fingers graze the inside zipper partition. Camille's name pops up on the video call app. I glance at the time before I accept the call.

"Did you bug my things?" I ask.

"There's a thought. I'll make sure to do that next time, sha. I take it you're in your hotel room and about to settle down?"

"That was the plan. I have a few hours before the night's activities."

Camille brokered an invitation for me to Covo del Peccato—Gio Oliveri's exclusive sex club. Another lost bet or was it a dare? All the same, when will I learn to avoid Camille when she gets that sparkle in her eyes? That woman knows how to phrase a dare and make a bet that gets me to rise to the occasion.

Every goddamn time.

She knows it's the only way to get me to do something I don't want to do. As strong-willed women, it has benefited our club, but that doesn't mean we don't chafe against each other. We are bosses in our own rights and taking a back seat to others sometimes feels alien.

"You better do me proud. It took a lot of convincing for Gio to agree to a meeting and I think he's testing us with this club invite."

"Hold up, does he expect me to have sex there?"

"As far as I know, *he* doesn't expect shit."

"Cammy, please tell me you aren't over there trying to pimp my pussy out."

"Someone needs to." Cammy's eyes travel up and down the screen, passing silent judgment on my clothes. Thanks to my jewelry and makeup, my leather jacket, white tank top, and cuffed shorts, which would look too casual on someone else, are glammed up on me. "Your bike is no substitute for good hard dick," she says, unable to find fault with my attire.

"If that's the only reason you got me going to this club, I

might as well relax until Monday." If pulling out my laptop to monitor my cargo business is relaxing, then that is what I'll do. My company has been growing since the day I unloaded my first shipment. I have great employees, but ships dock all hours of the day and I like to keep tabs on everything. Moving shipping containers is a dangerous job, even with all the safety checks I've implemented.

"Yo ass knows better than to slack off. If Gio shows up, it will be a great opportunity to soften him up for the hard sell during business hours. You can't risk him not being there. The worst that'll happen is he doesn't show and you have a fun night, preferably with a lot of dick."

I glare into her smug face. "Remind me again, why are we pushing to get into business with this man?" I ask while I unpack the rest of my clothes, including my power suit for my sit-down meeting with Gio. "From everything Owl put together, he's a misogynist. He doesn't work with women."

"That's not entirely accurate. He has a good track record for his legal enterprises. That's why you need to turn on the charm and make him understand what a gem your cargo company is. But not too much. From my call with him, he doesn't react well to pandering."

"Good, because I don't pander." Flossin' on Stiletto wHeels is our holding company, but my cargo company, Z. Roudanez Coastal Cargo, is a subsidiary. It's one way we continue to consolidate wealth within our family.

"Give him some of that New Orleans sweetness and you'll be good. A win with him will go a long way for our Flossers. We'll be the first woman-run organization the Oliveris recognize. And if things go our way, even Daddy will have to stop patronizing 'our little hobby.'" Camille's eyes gleam.

Daddy's acknowledgment means a lot to both of us. He "allows" us to operate separately as a club because he expects us to fail. It's his damn fault all his daughters are in the life, but his club has always been hostile to women riders. And to be honest, Cammy and I hate the way they treat women who haven't earned their "Old Lady" badges. This is why, when Cammy first proposed the club, I was all for her. Then she drew up the founding documents and surprised me with the VP and co-founder title. Did I mention, we never discussed me being anything more than a member? It has been five years, yet I still get drawn into her schemes. I wish I knew how to stop her before her outlandish ideas come about.

"Now, about tonight. Show me the outfit."

I roll my eyes and get off the bed. "I do know how to dress myself. I've been doing just fine for twenty-eight years."

Since I turned four, actually. The morning after I blew out my birthday candles, I informed *the* Mrs. Maxine Roudanez I would decide on my outfits from now on. Shock was only the first emotion that crossed her face. She mistakenly thought I was kidding, but I knew my mind then, just as I know it now. But I allow my sister to believe she can dictate my wardrobe. No matter what she says, I'll wear what I planned on wearing. I do not engage in frivolous arguments.

"Uh-huh. I'm not about to let you walk up into that club with 'just fine.'"

I point the camera at the red off-the-shoulder dress. With cutouts on the sides and a long slit to my hip, I will have a lot of skin on display, and no panties to ruin the dress' impact. I pray the wind doesn't kick up tonight. The last thing I need is to get arrested for indecent exposure. Next to the dress, I place my six-inch red bottom heels.

"At least you understood the assignment with the dress. Now, how you doin' your hair?"

I roll my eyes. "Do you not see these fresh passion twists I'm rocking?"

"I do. They cute, too. But, again, how you doin' your hair?"

"If you don't get off this phone with your nonsense. I have a plan for hair and makeup. I always do."

"Hmm. I want to see it put together. Send me a selfie before you leave. And if they allow you to keep your phone while you're in the club, I want to know what Gio offers. Who knows? I might be tempted to visit if you cinch this for us."

"Smoke must not be around. If he ever heard you talking about what Gio offers, he'd be dragging you off the phone to do all manner of things my innocent eyes and ears don't need to witness. He'll have you forgetting Gio's name in no time."

Although I'm not Smoke's biggest fan, I support Cammy's choice. Something about the way he treats Cammy rubs me the wrong way, but until he does something that necessitates a Roadanez beat down, I'll leave him be.

"You haven't been innocent for a minute, but you right. I should have this conversation at Smoke's place. No probs, I'll find a way to bring up where you're headed tonight. And please, don't automatically say no if a hot guy approaches you. Take a night and enjoy yourself to the fullest before you come home. In fact, when I call you in the morning, please let your mystery man answer the phone. You know I can tell if he put the work in by his morning-after voice."

"You outrageous. I'm hanging up now."

"Fine. I guess I'll listen to your voice. If he did his job, you won't have on—"

I hang up on her. If she catches me laughing, it will only encourage her. I order room service. Instead of pulling out my laptop and working, I relax while envisioning the night ahead. Truth is, I've never been to a sex club. What research I found on what to expect still left me uncertain; there is plenty of variety out there.

Is Oliveri's club safe? Will there be leather, chains, and whips everywhere? Red and black walls with strobe lights making it hard to see and easy to remain anonymous? Will people be fucking on every surface? Just thinking about the possibility of naked limbs, pheromones perfuming the air, and gyrating hips, has my pussy throbbing. Wetness seeps onto my thighs.

Damn Cammy for turning my thoughts onto my neglected body. After eating a light meal of grilled shrimp, roasted asparagus, and mashed potatoes, I jump into the shower. The cool water does nothing to dampen this nameless need clawing at me. My skin is too sensitive, and the showerhead does not detach.

Fuck it.

I rinse off and jump out, knowing I will take a second shower before I get dressed. Inside my suitcase, there is a travel pillow. Meant for discretion while going through TSA, it is the perfect pouch for my O-makers. When a girl needs to take flight, she keeps her options open. Toys in hand, I settle on the bed and close my eyes. A film roll of faceless, hot bodies plays behind my lids. Their muscles bulge and my pussy throbs in response. I am in no mood for long and drawn-out play.

I start the vibrator on the lowest setting to accustom my clit to the new sensation. The first contact is the best. It thrums through my entire body, a forewarning followed by intense shocks accompanying every soft vibration. Gradually, I increase the frequency. There is no controlling the wetness pouring from my nether lips. I slip my dildo inside me, giving my pussy what she needs, thrusting it in and out, squeezing the hard silicone inside my walls. Frantic, I increase my speed.

Visions of a faceless shaved brown head between my thighs spur me higher. Tension fills my body. I clench my teeth to hold in my whimpers, but I am so gone I have no idea if I succeed. This is a classy establishment, and I am a fucking lady. My hotel neighbors need not hear me fucking myself enthusiastically enough for my screams to shatter glass.

And I almost do. Shatter glass that is. I needed that O more than I realized. Lethargy steals through me, my legs flop to the side, and my breaths come in short pants. If I ever find a man that can do that for me, I will reconsider the need for my toys. But this man, this figment of my imagination, has a long way to go before I set aside my O-makers.

Cammy's earlier needling is only partly to blame for the need overtaking me. I haven't had a good dicking down in too long. Most men I meet have a problem with taking direction in the bedroom. And I am too knowledgeable about my body's needs to be some man's test drive. My phone's alarm blares an alert. It's time to get ready for my night out. Hopefully, this session will get me through until I return.

But thinking about all the possibilities at Covo del Peccato is enough to send me into a cold shower. I clean my toys, certain they will be put to good use when I return.

CHAPTER TWO

Zaïre

*M*iles outside of Felicidad proper, the driver passes acres of remote land. There are no neighbors over the horizon in any direction and no cars that I can see. Am I about to get a private tour? Or is something more sinister happening?

I pat my clutch, assured that my discreetly designed tactical survival pen sits comfortably in my silk-lined bag. Anyone thinking they can get the best of me will find that Jason Bourne isn't the only person who knows how to pen them to death.

My hired car pulls up to a nondescript building. A Romanesque perron leads to the front door one story above the ground. Circling the foundation are needle palm trees. In front of them, pink, purple, and red trumpet-shaped coral creepers spill over their urn-shaped containers and perfume the air with their sweet scent.

Oliveri offered his car and driver, but like his offer to put me up in a hotel, I declined. I believe that when I'm on someone else's turf, I must maintain as much power over my surroundings as possible. As well-manicured and landscaped as this property is, I am happy Mr. Oliveri has no say in when I can leave his establishment.

I climb the impressive stairs and swipe a keycard over an invisible card reader per the instructions given to me before I left New Orleans. The door immediately opens, and I step forward with a confidence I don't entirely believe and wonder what this new experience will unfold. A uniformed attendant meets me at the entrance. Nothing on this floor reads sex club. Neutral tones surround me. From the Greek columns, plush runners over Italian marble, and the soothing landscapes on the walls. This dichotomy unsettles me, but I betray none of my unease.

"Ms. Roudanez, my name is Paolo. I will be your attendant this evening. Please surrender your phone. We will return it to you on your departure."

I hand him my phone, having expected the request. From what little Oliveri provided about this place, the first, second, and third rules are all about circumspection. Paolo also searches my clutch and returns it to me without confiscating any items.

"Mr. Oliveri requested I provide you with a tour unless you know the variety of entertainment in which you wish to indulge tonight?"

"Hmm, what's available?"

"Follow me. We pride ourselves on discretion. If, during your stay in Felicidad, you require our services, we have a reservation option where you may special order the experience you wish to be fulfilled." He points toward a wing to the right. "The upper levels and rooms down this hall are equipped with everything you may need, and they are sound-proofed for your privacy."

He leads me to an elevator off the left wing. The rug muffles our steps.

Damn, this place gives off Old World vibes. And how many people are fucking to need three floors dedicated to their deviant asses? Maybe this is how people in Felicidad introduced flavor into their lives.

"Downstairs you will find the public pleasure rooms," Paolo says. His words slip through me and paint images of leather, chains, and naked men and women indulging in debauchery.

My nipples peak, my excitement undeniable. Anticipation chases away my disquiet. We descend, and the doors open to a hedonistic world that accomplishes the impossible, marrying class and raw sex. It is a union of sensualism and intimacy that has me panting, needling me to indulge if even a little. The patrons mill about, not as deep into the kink life-style I studied in preparation. Yes, there are leather-clad men and women, chains, and collars but nothing is overdone, and everything ratchets up the heat pulsing in my body.

The entire floor is an open concept with sheer curtains cordoning off areas. Everything is smoky gray and purple, very different from the neutral interior upstairs. Dim lighting lends to the loss of inhibitions. Even the smell. *Fuck!* Has Oliveri discovered, bottled, and diffused the perfect pheromone to drive everyone wild with lust? I can't get enough of the enticing scent.

Off to my right, barely shielded by the sheer curtains, a woman stands before a blindfolded man strapped to a St. Andrew's cross. The flogger in her hand and her serious demeanor are at odds with her gauzy pastel pink dress. The man whimpers, then thanks and begs her to punish him more.

On my immediate left, a throuple ignores everything around them. The redheaded man is naked while servicing two sinfully dressed women at their direction, one blonde, the other brunette. He is easily twice the width of his female companions, and if he were to stand, he would tower over both of their petite frames.

The brunette orders him to do something. My distance and the sensual music playing from invisible speakers prevent me from overhearing her. But there's no need for me to get closer to understand what was said. The redhead begins sucking on the brunette's toes. It must be something she enjoys, her head falls back and her mouth opens on a gasp. The brunette's mouth moves again, and the man slowly licks and kisses his way up the blonde's thighs.

This is not a new experience for them. I am a stranger watching them for the first time, but their comfort with each other emits a palpable energy reaching across and bathing me in the moment's sensuality. The brunette pulls the blonde's thighs open. Like me, she has foregone underwear, her arousal glistens at me across the room, shiny and wet. The brunette kisses Blondie's exposed neck, and the redhead finally reaches the apex of the blonde's thighs. Both women begin to instruct their male companion whose head bobs gently between spread thighs while the two women engage in a passionate kiss. Pride and growing pleasure peek through the smiles on the women's faces when they break to admire the man diligently applying his mouth.

Where do I find a man who delights in taking instruction so well?

"Would you prefer to explore on your own?" Paolo asks me in a whisper.

I nod, unable to take my eyes off the throuple.

"I am at your disposal if you have questions." He presses a small square device into my palm.

I study it, then test it by depressing the surface and a low buzz emits from his breast pocket.

"Whenever you page me, I shall find you," he says, then boards the elevator.

Having peeled my eyes off the three people, I now take the time to absorb the surrounding activity. I wander the floor, catching glimpses of naked breasts of all sizes and builds. My body begins to overheat from within. The visual stimuli have made me slick with lust with no one to slake it on.

How long can I survive before wanting to indulge or needing to escape to my hotel and my O-makers?

I almost forget I am here to take advantage of Mr. Oliveri's hospitality. If I can find him and lay a foundation for my pitch come Monday, I'll have satisfied part of Cammy's request.

Although, with the way my pussy is leaking, I might satisfy her more outlandish request, too.

In the middle of the floor, a group of people has congregated in a circular curtained "room". Curious, I join them. Until I am convinced Gio Oliveri will not make an appearance, I will remain. My O-makers and my pussy will suffer the consequences later.

The only available seat is an empty half of a daybed next to a gorgeous specimen of a man. My clit throbs from my first glance. Is he here for similar reasons as me, to explore something new? Or is he a regular?

He has an air of speculative amusement. As if the twenty people in various states of coitus on the surrounding daybeds have nothing new to entice him. He wears his experience as well as he wears his casual suit, fitted like a second skin. Something tells me he will blend in in almost every environment. Upper class like this, but even somewhere as gritty as my daddy's club.

The first four buttons of his shirt are undone, granting me a peak of the hard muscle underneath topped by a soft mat of hair. His blond hair falls away from his face in an effortless, just-out-of-bed appearance. How my fingertips tingle. I want to run my hands through his locks and take my time with his body. Shit, I want to lay him flat and use him until I come.

Please let him be like the man in that throuple.

I doubt it. His confidence exudes power. He isn't the type to take a backseat to anyone. I sigh in regret but continue to admire the stranger's looks. In the dim light, I can't tell what shade his eyes are, but they are a light color. He turns those mysterious orbs on me, ensnaring me, drawing me closer until my ass lands on the daybed without conscious thought. His lips quirk to the right revealing a hint of a dimple.

This man!

The hint of disinterest disappears as his eyes slowly sweep up and down my body. Damn if I don't feel it on every inch of my skin. And there is a lot of skin. I am a thick woman, with three c's thiccc. Hence, it takes a while for him to get to my bare hip and the side peak of my ass.

I rub my damp thighs together. Based on the flare of his nostrils and the admiration in his gaze, this man appreciates what he is seeing as much as I do. But he's probably used to dictating what happens in the bedroom.

My need is getting out of hand. I will absolutely need a partner to work off this frenzy building inside me. But my body refuses to follow my mental directions to look else-where for my entertainment. I am entirely too focused on my daybed companion that I almost miss the flurry of activity from the surrounding loungers. Everyone turns their attention to the new couple heading to the center platform. Everyone except my daybed partner. When I finally turn to watch what the other couples are intently staring at, I gasp in recognition.

There will be no approaching Mr. Oliveri tonight. His wolfish expression has one target: his wife. With riveted attention, I watch as Gio's wife melts as he whispers in her ear. Are they filthy? Cruel? Sweet? Not that it matters.

The world disappears, except for the distractingly sexy heat generator beside me, and I become an invisible spectator to Gio and Jessie Oliveri's love fucking. Although I can see the affection shining through their eyes, what they do on that bed isn't lovemaking. Intimate but not sweet and a thousand times hotter than an inferno. My body is on overdrive, and I need relief.

Warm air touches my ear and I shiver.

"Sweetheart, a woman like you should never be left in this much want," my companion says. His deep raspy voice has a Texas drawl that goes straight to my pussy, and I swear my ovaries drop. "I'll give you what you need and make sure you walk out of here satisfied. *If* you manage to walk after I'm done with your pussy."

I swallow. Hard. Because as much as I know we will clash, my body doesn't give a fuck. My pussy wants him. I keep my eyes on the naked couple in the center fucking like there aren't a ton of people watching and getting off on them. Jessie rides Gio in a reverse cowgirl while his fingers splay her pussy lips wide for everyone to see his dick pump in and out of her. My pussy clenches in response.

I scrounge up enough words to string together a coherent thought. "Brave words from a man that doesn't know my pussy has superpowers."

"Is that right?"

I arch my brow at him and manage to hide a smirk.

"I guess this makes my cock the supervillain, known for destroying worlds and devastating lives."

"Who will win, Super Pussy or Super Cock?"

His tongue pulls my earlobe into his mouth. "Although I've got the kryptonite to make Super Pussy weep, I think we'll both leave here winners."

I turn my head, reminding myself to breathe and regain my equilibrium. This man's wit and filthy words are just as arousing as the pretty picture he presents. The problem is everything my eyes fall on makes me want to put his confidence to the test.

An attendant appears beside me. It's not Paolo, but someone else in a similar uniform. He looks at the man beside me in polite inquiry. Then my companion touches my back. My naked skin bursts to life, and I gasp. He grins and I glare at him.

"Let's follow the nice gentleman here, then I can take care of that sweet pussy you're hiding from me."

I cut this gorgeous motherfucker a glance sharp enough to slice through a mountain. It's the look I have given to men who believe they are more...everything. More knowledgeable. More desirable. More proficient when it comes to me and my body than I am. They usually slink away with the new understanding that they are not as grown and worldly as they think they are.

Not this man. This man dares me with an upward tick of his lips and the hint of a sexy dimple. And to be honest, it turns me right the fuck on.

I should walk away. When will I learn my lesson about accepting dares? Not tonight, apparently. Not while I'm sitting here hot, wet, and wanting with a man more than willing to at least take the edge off. What's the worst that can happen? I get a small O, return to my hotel and take care of myself.

As if sensing my capitulation, he stands with his hand outstretched. I let the slight frisson of annoyance go and place my palm in his. His hand dwarfs mine. Hell, now that we are standing so close to each other, everything about him dwarfs me. I blame it on the dim lighting and my big ass' ability to act as a booster seat. Were his shoulders always this broad?

We follow the attendant to the upper floors, but I am not paying much attention. We could be going to a different building for all I care. My heart is beating a wild anticipatory beat, and my pussy is dripping down my thighs—if I'd worn panties, they would be ruined but at least then I wouldn't worry about leaking all over the floors. I came unprepared.

We are given a private room. Along the walls are built-ins. Are these rooms where they hide the kinkier toys? It's neither here nor there. I don't use other people's toys. I'm rather vanilla with a need to orchestrate my pleasure. Soon after entering the private room, the attendant returns with fancy finger foods and champagne. He leaves, and I head to the glasses, needing something to replace the moisture that has disappeared from my throat.

He beats me to it and fills a flute for me. Was his purpose to keep me unbalanced? Needing to establish my authority, I sit in the armchair, a makeshift throne to show him who is calling the shots tonight. I spread my thighs enough to let my dress slip between them, but not enough for him to glimpse my treasure. His eyes widen the moment he sees the glistening sheen on my thighs. He walks over to one of the built-in drawers.

"I don't play with other people's toys. Only mine touches my pussy," I say.

He pulls out the drawer and rifles through the contents ignoring my statement. He turns with a sleeve of six condoms and a wicked grin. "Sweetheart, when I'm done with you, I'll be the only toy you need in that pussy."

Too much air travels down my airways on a desperate

inhale and I cough, then take another sip of the crisp champagne. But the coolness sizzles to nothingness.

Why is it so hot in here? Invisible steam escapes my body, but there is no relief from the heat that continues to build. I drape my legs over the arms of the chair and flip the skirt of my dress, providing an unobstructed view.

His steps falter. If I hadn't been watching closely, I would have missed it.

It is my turn to smirk. "I want you on your knees."

The closer he gets, the higher my anticipation grows. I'm impatient to see him between my thighs with my hands clutching his hair as I ride his tongue to completion. My hips arch in his direction as if he is a powerful magnet and I, a lowly metal screw. He reaches me. His legs press against the chair.

"All in good time, sweetheart. I'm fixin' to taste your mouth first." He bends and scoops me from the chair.

I am in the air before I can respond to him. Me and my big ass. Lifted like I'm a small child. He is the first to attempt it, and I don't recognize this fluttering inside my belly. The man doesn't even have the decency to act like he overestimated his ability. But that's a good thing, right? It means his physical strength can match mine. It also means he thinks he can treat me like some petite little thing he can bend any which way.

I open my mouth to tell him about himself. "Mph."

Instead of words coming out, his tongue invades. And he does not try to hide his intention. He means to conquer my depths. He overpowers my tongue, eviscerates the bubbly champagne flavor and replaces it with his own. Wild and domineering and so much man that I struggle to counter him. A small voice inside me demands that I lay down my arms and surrender to his mastery. And though I hate the idea of submitting to anyone, this kiss is the best I've ever experienced.

Will he do to my pussy what he is doing to my mouth? My center clenches at the thought, eager for him to begin.

CHAPTER THREE

Lucien

*T*his sultry siren's mouth has distracted me since the moment she sat beside me downstairs. Between the sass she dished out and the wickedly sharp intelligence shining through her eyes, she hooked me before our lips touched.

I may have led her to the room, but she's the one controlling my actions, my inability to ignore her and walk away. The reason I came to the club was to observe, nothing more.

Her bossy directives are a challenge I'll not ignore. Who would forego the chance to tame and corrupt Super Pussy? Not me. Even if I fail, I bet I'll never be the same.

I swoop in for the taste I've been curious about, my patience at an end. She explodes on my tongue, champagne, heat, and a flavor so rich and complex it's gotta to be all her. It's a flavor I can't get enough of.

Like my conquering ancestors, I pillage. I thrust my

tongue inside her mouth, marking every crevice as mine. Because by God she will be. She can't tease me with her flavor and expect to walk away. Not from me.

Fuck that.

I won't let her go when each taste of her whispers across my tongue that this woman belongs to me. I don't care how brief our conversation, she calls to something soul deep inside me.

A growl escapes. I think it's mine until she asserts herself in this communion of lips and tongue. I smile as she nips my lips. At every turn, she attempts to top me and demonstrate her strong will.

She has yet to realize that I'm the apex predator. The one who hunts and devours the other dangerous predators people fear. Upon first meeting me, everyone recognizes the threat resting just below the surface. Not my sultry siren. She's fearless, a good match. I'll enjoy teaching her everything she needs to know about me.

I stiffen my tongue and overpower hers once more. She's had her moment. Tonight's all about me and the many ways I'll make her come for me. On my fingers, my face, my cock. I lower her to stand on her legs and capture her face in my hands to deepen the kiss that I don't want to end. If the building were to combust, I wouldn't give two shits, happy to kiss the ever-loving fuck out of my siren.

When the need for air becomes too powerful, I break the kiss. Her plum-colored lips are swollen to nearly twice the size, her pupils are blown, and I swoop in for another taste. This time I suckle. Her lips were juicy before I began mauling her mouth, they are even sweeter now that my flavor has intermingled with hers. My cock is so hard, I want inside her.

Now.

I unzip her dress and unsnap her bra, our mouths still connected.

Her neck, the smooth column of her skin, taunts me. It's my next destination. I tilt her chin, sucking, licking, and kissing her deep red-brown skin. Beautiful and unblemished. I nip and suck harder. Yeah, I want to mark her, give her a constant reminder of this moment. She moans, the sound connecting with my cock. I have never been this possessive of someone in such a short time, but philosophical thoughts about the primal reaction she brings out in me are for moments when I'm alone. Not when I have a gorgeous woman built to take the type of fucking I need at my fingertips.

My siren hasn't melted into me completely yet. She still resists my lead. It will make the moment she surrenders to me all the sweeter. She clutches at my hair. The sting from her grip makes me harder. Sexy, ferocious growls interrupt her moaning as if she is withstanding the overwhelming pleasure I am giving her through determination. No matter. I will turn her snarls into purrs soon enough.

I move to her breasts. There is nothing about this woman I dislike. She has a pear shape, with wide hips and ass while her breasts are small, for her size anyway. They are still more than a mouthful. Perfect for me.

She pushes me away when I am millimeters from engulfing her nipple. "Let me see what you're working with. I can't be the only one standing naked in this room," she pants.

I hesitate, debating whether to ignore her directive. I give orders. But I will take this as a suggestion, one I don't mind following if it means more skin-to-skin contact. I divest myself of my clothing, smiling at her gasp and the daunted look on her face as she stares at my cock. I harden further, my length rising in response to her reaction; incredible as I was already hard enough to hammer nails. She licks her lips and wetness seeps from my tip.

Yeah, I'll feed her hunger there, too.

Her knees begin to buckle.

Not yet.

I grasp her elbow and walk her to the bed, pushing her gently on top. I retrieve a condom and sheath my cock. The rest I toss on the bed. "Sweetheart, now's a good time for your pussy to get right with God."

"You talk a big game, big man." She raises herself onto her elbows. "I evaluate performance, and you have a long way to go before anyone begs for divine intervention."

A laugh escapes me. My siren's humor is refreshing, another way she matches me. I stroke my cock and squeeze the tip. Fuck, this woman has me ready to blow, and I haven't been inside her yet.

"Why don't you put that mouth of yours to better use?" She spreads her legs for me.

I lick my lips at the fluid shining on her skin. Her pussy, a deep, glistening pink surrounded by her dark brown skin is the most gorgeous fucking sight I've ever seen. Her fore-finger snakes its way into her trimmed curls, not stopping until she spears herself.

If she thinks she'll fill her body better than I can, her eyes aren't working. I don't take too kindly to people doing my job for me. I grasp her wayward hand and bring it to my lips.

"Tonight, this pussy gets what I give her, if and when I decide to give her anything. And this…" I suck her fingers of all her sweet, salty juices one by one until only her natural taste remains. "Has no business inside her tonight."

She moans at the suction. Her hand goes directly to my cock, but I twist and block her from touching me yet. Once I've fucked her a time or two tonight, I'll allow her the opportunity. Two times should be enough to no longer need to bury myself inside her until I come from a glancing stroke, right?

I shake my head and return to the built-ins.

"I don't get a say in how I get off?"

I grin over my shoulder while I search. "Sweetheart, every moan from your lips is your say, and I'm an attentive listener." I quickly find what I need.

She eyes me as I return to her with a pair of silk scarves in my hand. "If those aren't for you, then—"

"We're going to address this habit you have of putting your hands where they don't belong." I interrupt, which silences her long enough for me to tie her to the headboard. My army training has a lot of perks outside the armed forces, but making knots and tying my siren in seconds surpass the rest of them by far.

Her stare runs my length, a curious anticipation behind her pretty hazel eyes. She doesn't fight or deny me, and her willingness makes her sexier the longer I'm in her presence because I know from our brief interaction, my siren can hold her own. Her sweet submission humbles me, but not for long. My need to be inside her is much greater.

"I enjoy hearing you talk sweetheart, so I'll keep your mouth free. That, and I'm going to tongue fuck your throat while my cock fucks the shit out of your pretty little pussy."

"Lord, Jesus." Her eyes dilate.

No other words pass her lips, but I read her shock and lust as clearly as if she is shouting it in my ears. I settle myself between her thighs and press my cock into the bed.

"Now, someone mentioned something about a better use for my mouth." I lean over her and take her nipple inside.

Her back arches and a gasp escapes her.

"I love how sensitive you are," I say between sucking her. "Do you have any idea how fucking beautiful passion looks on you? That's right, sweetheart. You're gorgeous and I can't wait to see how much more you can handle."

Not one to neglect a beautiful, unattended breast, I pinch and roll her other nipple, alternating the pressure to the sound of her breath catching. "Gentle and sweet? Or hard and relentless?" I ask around her hardened bud. I do it on purpose, of course. Any vibration on her sensitive nips is bound to produce the reaction I want.

"Gentle. I want gentle," she says.

"That's a shame. I'm in a real ornery mood tonight." I suck hard immediately after declaring my intent. "And your voice is so sweet, I want to hear you sing."

On cue, she trills, and her chest presses into my mouth.

I do the same to her other breast while paying attention to her body's signs. I've no doubt she knows what she likes, but a new man and a new touch can bring about new discoveries for her and her body. And as a born and bred Texan, I cannot in good conscience let a woman suffer from such neglect. It would be downright criminal.

Her body begins to shake. "Shit. No. This shouldn't be possible," she screams between breaths. Shortly after her mouth makes a soundless O, her head presses into the pillows.

My patience is at an end. My cock has been weeping to be inside her for too long. I crawl up her body and position my cock at her entrance.

"You did so good, sweetheart. Are you ready for your reward?"

She turns her disbelieving eyes to me; her breasts still trembling from her orgasm. Her mouth is too tempting. I don't wait for her response before I plunder her mouth and thrust into her at the same time. She drenches me as I glide in halfway with little resistance.

I swallow her surprised shriek. Even through the

condom, there is nothing but wet heat. She pulls at her restraints. Driven by a need for more physical connection, of her skin on mine more than anything else, I loosen the scarves and free her hands. She immediately encircles my waist, at first clutching then caressing me in a wild frenzy. It comes as no surprise when she rolls me onto my back and follows, our bodies still connected.

"My turn." She sits atop me, a goddess with flowing twists.

Her updo from earlier has collapsed and has become a living thing, writhing and swaying with her body, just as mesmerizing as everything else about her. She is the sexiest fucking woman to ever try and tame me. She seats herself fully on my dick, my testicles flush with her ass.

As if by silent decree, neither of us moves. We soak in the feeling of me inside her while she surrounds me. The moment passes and she winds her hips in a slow motion that will drive me insane if I let her continue for much longer.

"I've never come this fast before," she moans, swiveling her hips again.

The rhythm is frustratingly slower than before; a rhythm I currently don't control after willingly and uncharacteristically surrendering to her. My powerlessness is maddening, and not a state I'll remain in for long.

"Sweetheart, with me, you'll discover many new ways to come. Just you wait until I have you riding my hand."

Her pussy squeezes me. Whether it is a voluntary reaction means nothing to me. All that matters is that she looks forward to my domination again. Just as I'm looking forward to taking charge of her pleasure once more. I grab her waist above her thick, fleshy hips, loving the feel of her smooth skin in my hand, and I change her dance. No more slow grinding. I bounce her on my cock, enthralled as her breasts bounce with the force of my hips bucking inside of her.

Gotta get deep inside. Gotta get deep inside. The mantra is on repeat as I try to follow through. If I get deep enough, I can claim every crevice for myself.

Yes, I need her pussy to be mine. Not just for tonight. And I will do whatever it takes to get her to acknowledge it. I thrust in and out of her, my mind full of all the ways I want to fuck her, all the ways I will fuck her, and all the ways I'll relive fucking her. Fuck, I just want to be inside her pussy.

Her body begins to tremble again. Thank fuck, because I can't hold back much longer. I plant my feet flat on the bed and drive into her like my life depends on it.

She holds onto my forearms, screaming and moaning, "You feel s—so good. More. I'm about to come again, but I want more. Keep fucking me." She ends the last word with another shriek as her pussy convulses around my cock, trying to milk all my cum from my body.

She falls to my side, her eyes closed, a grin on her lips. I came like a bullet train, but that satisfied glow on her face has my dick reawakening. I discard the full condom and apply a new one. If I am going to have any chance of getting more days like today, I have my work cut out for me tonight. And I am a dutiful soldier.

She peaks at me with one eye. Her stare fixes on my cock bobbing up and down and pointing at her. "Already?" She turns on her knees as if to scurry away from me.

I grab her hips and pull them flush with mine. "Are you trying to tell me you don't want another go?"

"I—"

"Don't lie to me." I cup her pussy. Still drenched. Still needy. She moans and her hips move in tandem with my caress. "I'll make you reveal the truth whenever you do."

"Fuck, I shouldn't. You were the one who should be on your knees waiting for me to tell you what to do next, yet I'm the one wanting more and willing for you to do anything. This isn't right, but—"

"No buts. You want to fuck me, and I absolutely want to fuck you. Now kneel for me like a good girl, and I'll take care of you."

"Who the f—"

I spank her ass. Not hard. Enough to have her flesh jiggling and my cock throbbing for another go into her heat. Enough for her to bend and moan her need without further complaints. I position myself behind her, my hand on her nape. "You're going to wish you never asked me to be gentle," I whisper into her ear. I slowly enter her body. The tease she tried to put on me earlier, I give to her tenfold. Pushing and dragging my dick along her sensitized canal. "And if you think for one second you can touch what's mine without my permission, I have the scarves ready to prove you wrong."

"But my clit. I need to rub it."

"Wrong. You need me to rub it. It's my clit to take care of from now on."

"You're—"

"Sweetheart, if I need to put a gag on you because I don't like the words coming out of your beautiful mouth, I will."

When she nods and doesn't challenge me, I reward her with my finger on her clit. Her body jolts at the contact.

"See what happens when you let me take care of you?"

She nods with a groan as pleasure overwhelms her.

Slow, with gentle touches, I play with her button. It is with the same gentleness I push in and out of her. I keep a measured pace, embedding every sensation into my memory. Even the torturous tightening of my balls is insufficient incentive to quicken the pace. When I cum, it will be hard, furious, and with my siren.

Her body begins to show signs she is near. "Please, please, please," she begs.

No word has ever sounded sweeter.

"Okay, sweetheart. Come for me." I deliver a slap to her clit and it is enough to push her and me over the final hurdle into climax. Her pussy milks me of every ounce of cum I have, and we fall to our sides still connected.

I can easily call her body home.

I don't give my siren many chances to rest. When she calls for mercy, I soothe her sore pussy with my tongue and praise her with words. She soon forgets why she calls for leniency to begin with and begs me for my cock again. We repeat the cycle until she repeatedly cries for a rest, and I leave her body to cool on its own. I am desperate to make tonight last for as many days as I can. I start a new assignment next week, but I am willing to do long-distance. Anything, if it means I get to see her again. The feeling is only magnified when she turns to me in her sleep to rest her head on my chest.

I softly kiss the top of her head. A sense of completeness settles over me. Having my siren in my arms brings a sense of peace, like the cool breeze after a summer storm breaking a heat wave.

From our limited interaction, my siren does not share her inner self easily. Not in any meaningful way. But for me, she let her guard down a little. For this reason, when she burrows deep in my embrace, the thump in my heart is easy to decipher. I want her to let down her barriers with me.

It's on the tip of my tongue to wake her and demand her name, but that would violate the club's rules. As much as I want to say fuck it with Gio's rules, I won't. He is one of my most lucrative clients. His legal and not-so-legal businesses rely on my security firm for our IT specialization. I squeeze her to me. I will give her another hour before I give her more reasons to continue our liaison.

More than an hour passes by the time I wake up. From my body's reaction, I overslept, and it is probably mid-morning. I reach across the bed, my eyes still closed. Our combined smells, though on the brink of stale, are still better than waking up to coffee. The smile growing on my lips dies a premature death. She isn't here. Her side of the bed is cold.

I spring out of bed. All her clothes are gone. She left me with nothing, no note of apology, no souvenir. Her panties would have gone a long way to appeasing the beast inside me demanding that I get her back and never let her go, but I have nothing but an emptiness that wasn't there before I'd met her.

I don't question it. I know the signs. Damn near every Connors man for the past four generations has fallen as fast as I have. And everyone has not only gotten their woman but has maintained their happy marriages. I refuse to be an outlier. I must find her.

First, I need my phone.

I fight back anger and disappointment. How dare she leave when we're nowhere close to being done? We'll never be done. There's still a lot I don't know about her. Specifically, not exchanging names is the biggest thorn in my side. I don't mind calling her my siren; she is both mine and a siren, luring me with her sultry smile and challenging attitude to the sweetest death between her thighs.

I dress, barely repressing my frustration, and retrieve my cell. There is one man who can help me track down my siren. And I don't care how dangerous he is, what rules he has to break, or how it will affect my business. The only thing that matters is finding and teaching her why it's bad manners to walk out on a Texan who has claimed her as his.

CHAPTER FOUR

Lucien

*I*t's Tuesday afternoon when I step inside my house. The wave of relief I expect from being home doesn't hit me. It must be because my cat, Tux, hasn't run to the door to greet me with his needy meows. He is at Camille's. I debated picking Tux up on my way home, but my palace beckoned me not to detour because a stop at Camille's is never quick or relaxing.

After unpacking, I try to unwind from traveling by reclining on the couch and turning on the TV over my fireplace. I flip through the shows, but nothing grabs me. Frustrated, I turn it off and head to my kitchen. I open my pantry and fridge, probably a half dozen times, but nothing from the well-stocked kitchen interests me. Maybe if I'd stopped off at my sister's, I'd have found an outlet for this excessive energy.

Truth is, I'm restless. Have been restless since Saturday

night, or more accurately Sunday morning when I crept out of bed leaving the beautiful Texan asleep.

Damn, he was fine as fuck. And his voice! I can still hear him whispering his demands in that deep, molasses-coated voice he must have stolen from the devil himself. There was no other explanation for my uncharacteristic behavior, following his commands without protests and liking not being in the driver's seat for once. That and his dick game had me all discombobulated and shit.

I hesitated to leave. His sleeping face arrested me, drew me in closer. There was no hint of his devilish dimples. Those weapons should be outlawed for the safety of women every-where. I had no idea how lethal they were until he finally turned his full smile on me right before he wrecked me. Those dints and his bright, even teeth were irresistible and had me agreeing to shit I never would have allowed. Just looking at his chiseled jaw and its fine dusting of wheat blond hair had my sore and overworked pussy pulsing for one more go at him.

But it wouldn't be just one more.

He told me to prepare myself for more of the same from the night before and it was all too easy to envision it playing out. I had to bite my lip not to beg him for his name and number while he was inside me, driving me over the brink time after time.

What was the point? I don't live in Felicidad and cinching this deal with the Oliveris means other Flossers will liaise between our organizations. It was best not to prolong our interlude. Best not to think past getting my ass back to my hotel room.

I made the right decision. Or at least I started to believe I had after repeatedly telling myself I had. I used preparing for my meeting on Monday as a distraction, losing myself in Owl's research on Gio and his associates, and the mutual benefits of doing business with Z. Roudanez Coastal Cargo and our transportation partners, all holdings under Flossin' on Stiletto wHeels. The prep time helped me focus and led to my successful meeting with Gio the next day.

Guilt, regret, and something else I can't name wash through me. Despite the rightness of leaving, I still slunk away like I was ashamed of what we did together. The least I could have done was thank him for a good time. It has been ages since I felt anything close to the satisfaction he delivered. Any more and I would have been comatose. It is too late to wallow in these feelings now that I can do nothing about them.

And as pleasurable as everything was, the domineering blond Texan scared me too. No man had ever taken charge of me and my body like he did. And I experienced things for the first time that…no. It's his possessiveness that sits at the top of my list. After a few minutes' acquaintance, he began making claims on my body. Had he not also voiced his intent, I would have still felt it in how he held and touched me. Three days have passed, and I still feel him nerve-deep inside me.

I'm a fucking womanist, independent, and have no time to be a man's trophy. No matter how tempting the picture we'd paint together, or how my heart thumps at the memory of his sexy drawl claiming me for himself.

I shake my head. I have shit to do today and dwelling on a stranger I'll never meet again is a waste of time that my practicality won't allow me to squander. I have been away from my office for three days.

Although I log into the system every day, nothing beats being on site in the thick of the controlled chaos inherent in loading and unloading cargo ships for their next destination. Maybe being in the familiar surroundings will finally free me of thoughts from this past weekend and wrangle this energy surge under control.

I decide to ride my Hayabusa. It's been too many days without her between my legs, hearing her roar in my ears, and riding through the open air. As I walk to my garage, my phone rings.

"Hey, Daddy. I was just about to head to the office."

"Don't bother. Ya mama nem expecting you, you heard me." The only reason Mama is expecting me this soon after flying in must be because he decided to have a family meeting. Otherwise, Mama expects me to see her when I'm well-rested.

"But I need to check—"

"It's important and can affect that little company you got, you heard me."

"I'll be there," I say, tamping down my knee-jerk response. I am so tired of this man downplaying my accomplishments. He's not playing favorites. He does this to my sisters, too. Although Cammy has gotten less of it since Smoke became President of the Bayou Hellraisers.

Sometimes I wonder if the only way we'll ever get Daddy's unconditional approval is to become a Bayou Hellraisers' Old Lady. Cammy is the only one of my sisters remotely close to getting that title. She and Smoke have been together for almost two years now, one year before Dad retired from the club.

Despite Daddy's lectures, where he displays his misogynistic tendencies, my sisters and I continue to pursue our personal goals. The Flossers wouldn't exist if we weren't silent rebels. We would be riding bitch to some Hellraiser, and even Camille doesn't do that for Smoke.

I've never told anyone, but I think the only reason Dad endorsed Smoke to replace him as president was because of his relationship with Cammy. I keep a lot of thoughts about my sister's man to myself. He might be family one day, and I don't need that kind of heat between me and my sister.

Smoke is too slick. He rose through the ranks at the Bayou Hellraisers fast…too fast. And although he is always courteous, I sense his true colors lie many layers deeper.

I take the I-10 for the thirteen-mile drive from Eastover to Fillmore. There is nothing like being in New Orleans, even if I'm driving through on the highway. There is a resonance to the city that anyone born here feels deep in their bones. Even as the city rebuilds and remakes itself, it will never be modern like Felicidad. There is too much history. And I live alongside it. With every breath, I inhale the struggles and accomplishments of my people, past and present. It is rich, flavorful and soulful, and there is no place like it.

In twenty minutes, I merge onto Paris Avenue and shortly after, I pull into my parents' driveway behind Jojo's bike. Thalie and Cammy's bikes are parked in front of ours blocking the two-car garage. From the coolness of the engines, they have been here a while. After sixteen years of my parents living here, the neighbors have accepted the slew of motorcycles that drop by at random times during the day.

Although they moved here while I was a sophomore in high school, the place never felt as homey as our house back in West Lake Forest. But after Katrina, Mama wanted bigger and newer. Daddy fulfilled her wish and bought her this place. Voices, plates clinking, and the smell of red beans and rice hit me the second I walk through the door. In the kitchen, I find my grandfather walking to the stove for what appears to be his second serving. He has good taste. My mama's cooking puts a lot of local restaurants to shame. I make the rounds, greeting everyone in the room.

"Komen to yê, Belzire," my grandfather, Guillaume, says as I kiss his cheek. "You break any hearts on your trip, sha?"

He is the only one who calls me Belzire, a Kouri-Vini diminutive for my name.

Pær Guillaume wants to keep the culture alive, which is why he only speaks Creole with us. There are days I want to ensure he accomplishes his goal, but my tongue never mastered the pronunciation, and I stopped speaking it altogether. I hope to one day pick it up again when I feel the sound of my voice won't disgrace my ancestors.

"I'm good, as are all the hearts I left behind. How 'bout you? I hear Ms. Bertie's still feeling some kind of way after she saw you stepping out with someone new."

"Wasn't no such thing. You know when you're second lining, the music takes your spirit. Ms. Bertie's just confused. Mo linm li konm ti koshon linm labou."

"I can't argue with how much pigs love mud, but I'd advise you not to say that in Ms. Bertie's hearing."

"Leave off harassing your granddaddy and get something to eat," my mama, Maxine, says.

Daddy comes strolling in from the backyard, casual as he pleases. His slow gait serves as a reminder that he summoned me to get here in a hurry. I tamp down a flare of impatience. There is food to be eaten and no business will be discussed until everyone has their fill—A Maxine Roudanez house rule.

Besides red beans and rice, there is fried chicken, cornbread, smothered okra, and corn maque choux. As I eat, Daddy periodically checks the time on his watch. He even walks out to the backyard again to call someone.

I motion to Cammy and then to where Daddy stands in front of the glass patio doors. He paces back and forth. Cammy shrugs, as do Jojo and Thalie. By the time I clean my plate, Daddy returns, a frown on his face.

"Let's all meet in the family room. Maxine, I'm expecting some guests. Let me know when they get here, you heard me."

"You expect them to listen to you on an empty stomach? In my house?" Maxine asks, her hands on her hips.

"I sure nuff do. You can hold off feeding them until after we're done talking business, you heard me." Daddy softens his demand by hugging her to his side and whispering something in her ear.

Maxine beams. Whatever Daddy whispers to her has her nodding. When she begins putting away the leftovers—food my sisters and I will take home with us—and putting a clean pot on the stove to prepare for these new folk Dad is expecting, I realize she agreed to relax her drilled-in-steel rule.

Jojo jabs my side. The jolt stops me from gaping at this phenomenon. At Daddy's grunt, Cammy, Jojo, Thalie, and I follow him into the family room where he stands in front of the entertainment center.

"Girls, I called you here because I got wind of some mess that might affect y'all and this little venture y'all've built."

"What you talking about?" Cammy asks. "We ain't heard nothing, and you know our contact, Shonda's ear is close to the streets. She knows what the cops are doing before they do."

"By venture, are you talking about our legal business or the other stuff?" I ask.

Although Cammy is our president, her immediate response seeks the fastest destination to an answer. Whereas I understand that going that route misses a lot of context. In our business, background information matters. It determines whether the one coming for our faces will finagle the law or work outside of it, whether our lives are on the line, our companies, or our entire club.

"When will you two learn to let a man speak? Make a betta example for your sisters, you heard me." Daddy points to Jojo who is sitting quietly and observing all of us. Not a lot gets past her. It's her most powerful trait. She folds her arms and leans back into the sofa.

"Sorry, Daddy," Cammy and I say together. We may be independent women and bosses in our own rights. But disrespectful? Never.

Daddy didn't become the president of the Hellraisers so that one of his daughters could shame him and cause his men to question his leadership. When a man's word means life or death, how his family responds to him is as important as the way the men he commands does.

His example drove Cammy to start the Flossers, for good or bad. Most of the uniqueness in our club is due to her recognizing that the same rituals in a man's MC wouldn't work for us. Her vision continues to draw Debutantes to join us and strengthen our group.

"Hmph," Daddy grumbles. "I got a tip-off that someone is looking to take over your territory and their first targets are you girls. Now, I know I gave my approval for you to branch off on your own with this hobby. Didn't think you would take things this far, opening up all these businesses and shit. Fact, is, I don't much care for what y'all've been doing, but I won't stand for nobody coming after my kin, you heard me."

"Who's your source?" Jojo asks.

"That's neither here nor there. And before you two interrupt me again, I've made arrangements for each of you. Until I figure out what's going down, y'all're getting private security. If y'all have a problem with that, keep it to yourselves. The man I hired is doing me a favor." Daddy stops to glare at Cammy and me. "And he's not from around here," he adds in warning.

I try to hold onto my neutral expression. His "warnings" are what I like to consider suggestions, but again, I won't throw my opinion in his face when there are other ways to get around him.

"Why can't we hire our own muscle?" Thalie asks what I assume we are all thinking.

Between the protection money and our various ventures, we have the funds and the pull to increase our security. Cammy runs combination dealerships and repair shops across the state, selling, fixing, and pimping domestic and international motorcycles. She is used to having security patrol the properties. Jojo has a tattoo parlor where her tats have become a mainstream staple for quality, original artwork here in New Orleans.

And Thalie...well, she's still figuring her shit out. She's more of a jack of all trades, doing stints in each company. Despite being the youngest at twenty, we've always encouraged her to make her own decisions. For us, that includes who she wants protecting her.

"I can probably trust you and Jojo to listen to your guards, but them bossy sisters of yours"—he points to me and Cammy while shaking his head—"I know them all too well. Don't give me those innocent eyes. You think because your security is on your payroll, you can ignore their advice. Well, you aren't the boss in this situation, and I made sure these men can't be bribed to look the other way—"

"Daddy, that happened one time, and I was in high school!" I interrupt, unwilling to let him exaggerate.

"You bribed your guards, too?" Cammy surprises me with her question. Not that it should. We sometimes behave too much alike for our own good. It's why we get along so well, but also why our arguments turn everywhere into a war zone.

"Yes, she sure enough did. And Zaïre's conveniently forgetting that her *bribes* weren't always monetary or relegated to high school, you heard me."

"You knew about those, too, huh?" I ask, avoiding eye

contact. "But were the others really bribes, though? One could argue—"

He twists his lips.

Hmm, I guess I wasn't as slick as I thought when I was younger. I turn to Cammy. "How'd you bribe yours?"

"Don't answer that, if you know what's good for you. You may be grown, but you still my kids, and I haven't forgotten how to discipline either of y'all. Hmph. Giving her ideas. Not today, you heard me," he grumbles.

My sisters and I fold our arms and arch our brows in challenge.

Jojo's quiet voice peeps out, "Who's telling Mama?"

Daddy drops his fierce expression faster than a blink. "Now, why you gotta bring her into this? You see? This why you need someone who don't answer to you protecting you. Y'all think you can just exploit any old body's weaknesses. Well, ain't no weakness to exploit with this group of men I hired, so your asses will be safe, you heard me."

The doorbell rings a brass band rendition of Whop Bezzy's "You Know I Ain't Scared." My mama's muted voice filters into the room as she greets the guests.

"Sounds like your security has arrived," Daddy says, peering through the archway.

I'm curious to see who Daddy has hired because I one hundred percent intend to run whoever it is in circles. It will take a strong man to get me to follow orders.

Now kneel for me like a good girl.

Fuck!

The memory of Saturday night's command whispers in my ear, and my pussy clenches as if missing the expected reward. I swallow. One night and that Texan has my body trained like Pavlov's dog. I really need to get to the office. Once I'm back to my routine, I will be better able to put this past weekend's activities behind me. I am so lost in thought that I almost miss the moment my world implodes.

Dwarfing my substantial mother is none other than Saturday's big Texan dressed in a sinfully tailored navy suit. My brain short-circuits. That happens when no coherent thoughts come through, right? Because right now, paralysis of the brain and body have to be the reason my butt is glued to the seat instead of… What? Hide like a little bitch? I'm not some hunted animal in a corner with nowhere to go. And he is no big bad wolf.

"Now kneel for me like a good girl."

I refuse to be the docile little partner from Saturday. If only my limbs would get the message and move. A need to escape the room overwhelms me, pumping blood through my veins, boosting my heart rate, and shortening my breath. All useless because I have not moved a centimeter from my spot on the couch since Daddy's visitors walked through the door.

Done with the niceties of talking with my daddy, Big Tex turns to the room. The moment he sets his sights on me, recognition sparks and a leonine grin spreads across his face that those dimples do nothing to diminish. Nope, he is not a wolf. He's the fucking king of the jungle. And he does not need to corner his prey. Not when he enjoys hunting quarry in the open. Not when he enjoys toying with his food before he pounces. And there is no doubt in my mind, he intends to play, pounce, hunt, and devour me.

"My siren," he says.

CHAPTER FIVE

Lucien

*A*s I stand in front of the home where I expect to get details into my next assignment, I breathe deeply. Ever since I woke up alone Sunday morning, I've been in a bad mood. The reason for my shitty disposition, I blame on my inability to find any clues about my siren's true identity. For the last three days, Gio has been less than forthcoming with information.

If I didn't know his people would detect my hackers, I would have had the information I needed on Sunday. But the Italian motherfucker didn't see me until Monday night. And something, maybe the almost imperceptible pause or brief tightening around his eyes, told me he knew who I was looking for, but no amount of negotiating on my part budged him.

Knowing this job with Hammer would further impede

my efforts nearly had me coming to blows with my brother Darren, who is also a silent partner in my security firm. Normally I would have delegated the task to another team, especially because Hammer had yet to explain his needs to me.

The door opens to a beautiful dark-skinned woman. Her upturned eyes remind me of my mystery woman. Is it wishful thinking? Am I seeing her everywhere because I am desperate to find her?

"You must be Lucien," she says.

"That's me. I also have my brother Darren, and two members of my team, Blake and Carter, with me." I point to each man.

All I knew before stepping through his door today, was Hammer needed at least four people and I had to be on the team. My people are pretty diverse. We represent operators from three of the five military branches. Blake is a muscular dark-skinned Black man who came to me after his enlistment with the Navy ended. Carter is Filipino and although he hasn't confirmed it, I'm pretty sure he's a fellow Delta Force operator.

We've all trained in hand-to-hand combat, have vast weaponry experience, and with Blake's expertise in mechanical and electrical engineering, we can build just about anything we need. For any type of digital intel, I have additional support back at the office. They'll be able to handle this job and the task that has occupied my every waking hour since Sunday morning.

Regardless of what I want to be doing, I owe Hammer. He saved my life and I believe in repaying my debts. It's why I agreed and boarded the plane, delaying my hunt for the siren who left me needing more.

Maxine leads me to a room off the entryway where

Hammer meets me. He grasps my hand and pulls me into a one-handed bro hug.

"My man, I'm glad you made it." Hammer stands at the entrance of what I assume is a family room.

I squeeze his hand and step back. "I had to wait for the rest of my exploratory team to arrive. We'll assess the situation and determine if we'll need more resources."

"Then let's get to it. I called in that favor so you can protect my girls." Hammer stares fiercely into my eyes. "There isn't much I treasure in this life. But when it involves my club, my wife, and my daughters, I ain't letting nobody mess with either, you heard me. And right now, there's a threat to everything I hold dear in my life."

"Understood, Hammer."

"I want your best, you heard me. I ain't looking for no budget security. I'll pay whatever needs paying for my girls. I chose you because I trust you. And right now I don't have a lot of that to go round. And my girls don't need to concern themselves until I've got a better handle on the situation, you heard me."

I squeeze his shoulder, understanding what Hammer really means. He intends to solve the problem currently endangering his daughters' lives himself. Adrenaline flows to my heart just thinking about the dangers. Threats I'll be staying away from with this stint because it is counter to why Hammer hired me. I swallow bitter disappointment.

I take risks for a living, have been doing so since my time in the Army. And I love every questionable situation I've ever encountered where there was no clear path to safety. If I'm not in one at the moment, I look forward to the next time, the next assignment I can insert myself into. The only exception was on Saturday night. The thrill I feel even now at the memory of holding my siren in my arms surpasses the Special Ops missions I've headed.

Although I'll not shirk on this assignment, I don't mind helping Hammer in resolving his situation sooner. "I can assign a team to you that specializes in intel gathering if you need," I say.

"I'll keep that in mind."

My team enters behind me, and I introduce them to Émile. They won't address him as Hammer until they've proven themselves. Hammer eyeballs them as if running a mental assessment of their fitness before nodding his head.

"Y'all just might do," he says.

I shrug away the momentary annoyance at his temporary lack of faith because his daughters' lives are at stake, and on some level, I understand him.

Émile pats my shoulder. "That ain't a reflection on your skills. I'm sure you'll handle danger just fine. But I have to warn you about my girls. Don't let their pretty faces fool you. They're wily and too independent for their own good. No matter what nonsense they throw your way, you stick with them, you heard me."

"Yes, sir," my team and I respond.

Silently I curb my impatience at the discovery that my new charge will be a handful. Immediately images of spoiled teenagers spring into my head. Although private security is many times glorified babysitting, it isn't actual babysitting. If I can, I'll supplement Émile's investigation so as not to shoot myself from the boredom of following some young miss around.

"Then I guess it's time I introduce you to my girls." Émile invites us deeper into the room. A contemporary take on classic furniture fills the space. Warm, neutral colors beg me to rest awhile.

Until my gaze lands on one of the room's occupants. My heart stutters before speeding like a runaway train. The woman who occupies my thoughts nonstop sits as if conjured by my prayers.

The foul mood plaguing me all day disappears the moment my eyes land on her. So much, I unconsciously blurt, "My siren." There's no context to the endearment I've been using for her since she turned my life upside down. Confused brown, hazel, and green eyes point my way, reminding me this is the first time I have uttered the words aloud.

But one pair of hazel orbs shows no confusion. A pinch of dismay and an entire serving of heat burns in my siren's glare. All appropriate reactions.

Set to stake my claim, Émile's voice preempts my first step in her direction. He introduces his daughters, but only one name holds my attention. Only one woman who has haunted me, her memory a bittersweet torture.

Zaïre.

Her name settles in my mind as beautiful as the woman herself.

We hold each other's gaze. Satisfaction, lust, hope, determination—they are all in the look I send her way.

"Darren, you're on Camille. Blake, you cover Jojo. And Carter, you've got Thalie."

My men nod and pass me to approach their new VIPs. We'll have to assess the Roudanez women's security needs based on their lifestyle. Once we've established our new routines, I intend to get more details from Émile about the threat to Zaïre's life. This assignment is no longer about a favor to a friend. It's personal.

Alone now that her sisters paired off with their close protection operatives, Zaïre storms over to me, but she keeps a safe distance between our bodies. A wise decision on her part.

"Let's get one thing straight, Tex—"

"Lucien."

She stumbles back on her heels but recovers almost instantly from my interruption. "I don't care how you know my father, you will not interfere with my life."

I close the distance between us until our toes kiss and whisper for her ears only, "You must need a refresher, sweetheart. From now on, I decide who and what interferes in your life. And if you need me to, I'll let everybody here know it, too."

As soon as she grasps my meaning, she frantically surveys the room. Our glances land on her father at the same time. Speculation furrows his brow.

"You will behave around my family," Zaïre hisses at me, a warm red undertone coloring her cheeks.

Émile claps his hands, gathering our attention before I can address my siren's challenge. It also serves as a reminder that Émile may object to my very unprofessional interest in his daughter.

"Now that y'all have met, let's continue getting to know each other in the kitchen." Émile ushers us through the house.

A spread of greens, cornbread, and a variety of delicious-smelling food is laid out buffet-style on the kitchen island. Maxine's food is worthy of my moving in and calling her Mama, but I'll never admit it to the woman who birthed me. A dish of barbecue shrimp that has no right calling itself barbecue has me moaning all kinds of undignified sounds. I would be embarrassed if not for the interest in Zaïre's gaze.

Once everyone has eaten their fill, my team gathers the necessary details from our new principals—addresses, phone numbers, itineraries, and anything else that comes to mind.

Émile clears his throat, gaining everyone's attention. "It's about time you folks think about on-site assessments. And girls, don't you go forgetting about what I done told you. Your money can't do shit for these men."

To reinforce Émile's message, I glare at each of my men. Blake and Carter nod, but Darren... He is staring a tad too intently at Camille. We may need to discuss what that look means in the near future. Brother or not, I will allow nothing to fuck up my plans for Zaïre or her safety.

Outside I begin to direct Zaïre to my car, as do the other men with their new clients. All protection vehicles in our fleet have reinforced armor and bulletproof glass. One by one the ladies divert to the four motorcycles in the driveway.

Not happening. I use my body to block Zaïre from mounting her bike.

"Your ride is over there." I nod to my car.

"Correction, *your* ride is over there. This is how I got here and this is how I'll leave."

Already we're at a standoff. All the sisters are. I peer into her determined eyes and weigh my options knowing my men will follow my lead.

"Now if you don't mind riding bitch, you're more than welcome to join me." Zaïre pulls a scarf from her helmet and wraps her crown.

"When we get to your place, we're going to have a conversation about acceptable behavior."

She opens her mouth to counter, but my forefinger on her lips stalls any protest. Her pupils dilate.

I laser in when a puff of air caresses the pad of my finger. Unconsciously, I circle the flesh, applying enough pressure to gain a small opening. As if by instinct, she licks her bottom lip and her tongue passes over my digit.

I cut the growl building inside me short and step away from the temptation she represents. We're still in her parent's driveway and I have no intention of giving her

48

father reason to suspect my very personal interest in Zaïre's wellbeing, but I won't deny it should he discover it.

I clear my throat. "For now, I'll follow you."

Suddenly a flurry of activity explodes around us. As if everyone was frozen in place until my words gave them the permission they needed. In my car, I wait for Zaïre to pull out while she takes a few moments to confer with her sister Camille.

Blake, Carter, Jojo, and Thalie turn off for their respective destinations, but Darren and I follow the two older sisters. I'm not sure what they are up to, but from the brief glimpse of my siren's personality from Saturday night, she is the type of woman to find solutions to her problems regardless of the men in her life telling her otherwise.

I find myself caught between admiration and exasperation at this quality. Women usually defer to me, but Zaïre will question and challenge me at every step. I can't deny the anticipation flooding my system at all the ways she will butt heads with me. The expected mental stimulation is as much of a turn-on as her body.

The four of us pull up to a quaint two-level Victorian home in Uptown. The address matches the one Camille provided earlier. Although visually appealing, this place will be a bitch for Darren to secure. Cars line the busy street facing the house and happy shrieking children playfully run down the sidewalks while dodging joggers and dog walkers. Darren has his work cut out for him.

At the front door, we are met with an increasingly demanding caterwaul.

"I don't know how he knows you're here. He *never* greets me this way." Camille retrieves her key to open the door.

"What can I say? He knows the sound my bike makes," Zaïre says.

As if by habit, Camille sidesteps the open door and a

black cat with a white tuft on its chest and paws runs to Zaïre and stretches to its full body length.

"I missed you too, Tux." Zaïre picks up the cat, which then clings to her in what I can only describe as a death grip around her neck. For an instant, I swear the miniature beast peeks through Zaïre's twists to give me the feline equivalent of a "hands-off" warning glare.

Camille leads the way into a deceptively spacious living room where she plops on a couch and stretches out. The furniture is a mashup of cold metals and warm fabric that shouldn't be feminine but is. Her love for motorcycles is everywhere, from the recycled parts displayed as sculptures on the brick walls to the stacked wheels as a center table. If Zaïre's passion for her bike is on par with her sister's, I'm going to have a bitch of a time establishing those boundaries I mentioned to her earlier.

Camille's cool gaze takes Darren and me in. "I know you technically work for our father, but if he ever catches wind of what we're about to discuss, we'll know you snitched. And we have our ways of making bitch ass snitches disappear."

"Sorry, and I don't mean to sound disrespectful, but can you hold off your discussion until we sweep the place? I'll make sure no one has been here to leave anything behind or is still here because I won't accept snitching charges if someone else is listening in." I glance at Darren who nods in agreement.

Camille and Zaïre share a speaking look before Camille agrees.

"Please remain here until we're done," Darren says. "If keeping your plan under wraps is more important than talking behind our backs."

My brother and I leave to go room to room. As we head down the hallway, my back itches. I don't have to turn around to know it's the combined pressure of Camille and Zaïre's glares drilling through our suits.

Darren's unnecessary dig should anger me. Getting on Zaïre's bad side will add obstacles to the future I'm trying to create. Instead, exhilaration fills me at the challenge, specifically how Zaïre will keep me on my toes.

Upstairs, I open the door to the main bedroom. Before I step inside, Darren pushes me to the side.

"I've got this room." He enters and shuts the door in my face.

I don't argue with him because It doesn't take a genius for me to realize why. Inside each room, we'll leave no crevice unsearched. And from the stares I've seen, Darren wants to protect Camille's privacy.

I enter another bedroom and pull out a small radiofrequency scanner. I use it to detect hidden recording devices and run it over every surface. Darren will do the same in Camille's room.

Once we confirm everything is clear upstairs, we repeat the process downstairs. The room the ladies occupy, we leave for last. Darren enters before I do and begins his scan. Tux hasn't stopped clinging to Zaïre since our arrival, and Camille leisurely sips from an old fashioned glass.

"Everything right as rain?" Camille sets her glass on the table beside her when Darren puts away his RF scanner.

"From what I can tell." I move to stand behind Zaïre. The need to be next to her is one I won't fight. Neither will I resist getting to know her better.

Darren stands across from Camille, his gaze focuses on her as if she is the only person in the room.

"I would offer you a sazerac, but you're on duty." Camille folds her arms. When neither Darren nor I respond, she straightens in her chair and points to two sets of documents.

"While you were upstairs, I put together a standard nondisclosure agreement you'll need to sign."

I read through the document thoroughly. In my line of work, it's standard for our contracts to include NDAs for our clients' protection. I'm sure Hammer would have requested one if he didn't consider the matter as urgent. An item referring to the Bayou Hellraisers' relationship with Émile catches my eye. Everything else references a motorcycle club, Flossin' on Stiletto wHeels.

Although I don't know all the details behind Émile's background, I've long suspected he wasn't just a recreational motorcyclist. Looks like his daughters aren't either. Camille's threat about snitches doesn't faze me, nor does this NDA. My client list includes powerful families with international reach.

Before signing, I glance at Darren. He nods, a sign he's fine with the contract. Satisfied that all the language pertains to keeping discussions confidential and won't hinder our relationship with Émile, I sign and hand my copy to Camille. Darren does the same, without breaking eye contact with Camille as he positions himself across from her.

"Now that the legal stuff is out of the way, I'd like to propose that we work together." My brother surprises me by offering the same deal I have in mind. "That way we all get what we want."

I peer at Darren more closely. He doesn't break his staring contest with Camille. If anything, his glare becomes more intense, confirming my earlier suspicion and potentially creating problems I don't need.

Fuck. Another Connors man bites the dust.

"Ladies, if you don't mind, I need to have a word with Darren before we agree to anything outside our duties or that will compromise our reputation with our client. Remain inside until we return." I grab my brother by the arm and drag him outside into the backyard. Once we clear the door, he snatches his arm from my hold.

"What the fuck Lucien?"

"Don't give me that shit. I'm not blind. I see the way you're looking at Camille." I keep my voice low to not carry to the neighbors or within the house. It won't do to expose my hand to Zaïre too early.

Darren walks away. "Yeah? How's that?"

"The same way I watch Zaïre. It's why I have an idea what's going on in that Connors brain of yours. But whatever you do, don't you fuck with my plans for Zaïre."

Darren returns to whisper, "Shit! Is she the one from—"

"You've been warned, brother. I can forgive you most things, but my future with that woman ain't one of them."

I don't realize how tense I am until his reluctant nod of agreement. "It's just as well. I don't know if you were listening closely while we were at Émile's because you were too busy drooling over Zaïre, but Camille's not single." He clenches his jaw at the distasteful knowledge. "I can't promise not to make a move, but I won't do anything that will cause her to interfere with you and your woman. Now as for whoever the man in her life is… I won't let him keep what's mine."

"He won't know what hit him." I shake my head. Neither will Camille. I pound my brother's shoulder. "We don't want to keep them too long. They're bound to start planning some objectionable shit. We need to make sure whatever they have in mind, we mitigate if not eliminate all risks involved."

"How can you be certain?"

"If you want to put money on it, I'm all for taking you to the cleaners."

"I'm good," he says.

We return inside in time to catch Camille and Zaïre sliding almost on top of each other as they skid toward the living room. With loud expulsions of air, they land on a different couch from the ones we left them on. Zaïre's cat isn't far behind. He furiously works all four legs to get to his owner, skidding into the couch at the last second. The sisters' rush is more revealing than words. My siren is curious about me. *Good*.

I'll satisfy all her questions in good time.

CHAPTER SIX

Zaïre

*C*ammy and I spy on the two ridiculously hot brothers from the kitchen window. When God decided on their gene pool recipe, He did not play. I swear He used DNA from Matthew McConaughey, Brad Pitt, and all the famous Hemsworth brothers for the express purpose of making all of womandom weep to touch their blond locks and hard bodies.

"You know Smoke's gonna shit bricks the second he sees who Daddy has guarding you."

"Smoke should know by now he's the only one I'm checking for." Cammy doesn't use the L-word. As much as I search my memory, I can't find one where my sister has ever professed to love… anyone, least of all Smoke. If only she would leave him.

I dismiss the thought. It has no bearing on our current

situation with the Connors brothers. "He might trust you, but I doubt Smoke'll trust Darren after he sees how intensely he watches you. By the way, where is Smoke?"

"I don't know. He said he wanted to be here to welcome you home, but with the emergency meeting at Daddy's place I haven't had a chance to tell him when you'd be here."

This news surprises me. I don't ingratiate myself to Smoke to warrant him thinking of me in his spare time. Instead of questioning his intentions out loud, I say, "It's just as well. I love entertainment, but I'm not sure I'm ready for the level of drama Darren and Smoke would generate."

"I don't know. Darren's got nothing on you and Lucien. Every time you get close there's so much heat between you two. It's like you know each other." She gives me a sidelong glance. "Well, have you met before?"

"Oh look, they're headed back." I avoid eye contact and rush to the living room, Camille and Tux on my heels.

Her body slams into mine and we drop onto different couches. "Don't think you can avoid me," she whispers low enough that the men behind us can't hear.

"I'm not. Promise. But now's not the time."

The truth is, I will tell Cammy about our one night together. I just haven't decided how much to divulge because my uncharacteristic behavior that night remains a mystery to me. And Lucien popping up when I thought I would never see him again is no help.

My sister settles herself on her chair, and Tux crashes his little on the furniture. The collision doesn't faze him as he leaps into the space beside me and sprawls half of his body on me and half on the couch. It always takes him a few hours to assure himself I haven't abandoned him after I've returned from a trip. I absentmindedly scratch his head.

"If we're going to find out who is threatening your organization, we should probably start with who you've pissed off." Lucien strolls into the room with a sexy swagger that reminds me of our night together. He dominates the space until I breathe only him. How is that possible when he's still half a room away? "From Émile's threat response, he isn't the only one who's rubbed someone the wrong way. Whoever is targeting you has a personal grudge. We'll go as far back as high school if need be. You'll be surprised how long some people will hold grudges."

"How did you know that's what we were going to discuss first?" Cammy asks, straightening her back.

"My brother can size people up pretty effectively, and he's got you two pegged as the kind of women who need to be in the thick of things," Darren says as he walks in behind Lucien and takes a seat across from us.

"Well, since we're of similar minds, let's begin." I pull out my phone and retrieve my running directory of adversaries. Not all of them have entered enemy territory yet, but if they keep underestimating my Flossers they'll force me to schedule their reckoning.

Suppressed amusement glimmers in Lucien's eyes. It's nothing I haven't received from my sisters. Camille rattles off a few more names that I inadvertently left off the list. To be sure we get everyone, I also text Thalie and Jojo for people we missed.

"Before we act on anything we find, my team is going to set up a security network connecting you and your sisters' houses. We have most of the equipment we need already. But now that we have an unidentified target, I'll be calling in for some more...specialized equipment." Lucien then lays out his plan on how to protect my family and search for the threat hanging over our heads.

For the first time since Daddy mentioned someone was

gunning for us, I examine my reaction. At the forefront is anger that someone would dare to threaten the Roudanez family. But the more Lucien speaks, the weaker that anger becomes.

Lucien has no problem bragging about his ability to tame me in bed, but when it comes to business, he exudes a calm confidence that needs no loud advertising. He commands the room without sucking up all the oxygen.

"What happens once we've identified the asshole responsible for this threat?" I ask.

Lucien shares a look with his brother who shrugs as if to say it's Lucien's call. "That depends. My team is experienced and works well together. You two are unknown entities, your skills untested. I'm inclined to keep you far away while we plant a trap"—He holds his hands up to stall the protest from leaving my and Cammy's open mouths—"But if during the investigation you prove yourselves worthy of the team, we'll include you in the final phases as well."

From the ferocious frown on Darren's face, he wasn't expecting Lucien's response, but he doesn't counter his brother. That's no sweat off my wig cap. I know when to lead and when to follow, though my first, second, and third choice is always to lead.

Hours into discussing our plan, Lucien stares out at the darkening windows. "Let's wrap up here." He calls for an end to the impromptu planning session. "With Zaïre riding her bike, I'd feel more secure about getting her home at a decent hour."

By the time we leave the house, the moon overlooks the streets. I dress Tux in his pink and rhinestone biker jacket and helmet and collect his custom cat carrier.

Lucien murmurs something to his brother while I strap Tux on my bike's pillion. As soon as I complete the task, I mount the bike and leave Lucien to catch up to me. He has my address and will eventually get to my destination. For now, I need the wind from the open road to clear my thoughts of the man who is bound to turn my life upside down.

✿✿✿✿

I'm sitting on my couch with a second glass of wine when the guard alerts me I have a visitor. I smirk as the memory of slipping between cars and leaving Lucien behind to maneuver through traffic in his big SUV overtakes me. Agility is one reason I choose to ride my bike more than any other vehicle.

With added liquid courage from the wine, I've convinced myself that Lucien's body wizardry from over the weekend has lost its hold on me. Unfortunately, drinking and the ride over aren't enough to make me forget the thoughtful acts he pulled during our talk. After clearing my throat once, I found a glass of water sitting in front of me. I stretched my neck for a second, and there was a pillow stuffed behind me.

One glance at Lucien told me the only thing holding him back from giving me a deep-tissue massage was to maintain some semblance of professionalism in front of Cammy. With no one living here with me, I doubt he'll be so circumspect. Either way, the thoughtful gestures cracked the shell I've surrounded myself with, and I need to spackle over it before it grows larger.

I release a breath and try to relax my muscles before approving Lucien's entry. I expect the mountainous man to burst through my door while raging at me, but the coldly efficient movements he greets me with raise the fine hairs along my body.

59

"Zaïre, sweetheart," he says, every muscle in his body under strict control as he approaches me.

As if by silent agreement my entire body mutinies at once and pulses in readiness the closer he gets.

Like a slow-motion sequence in an action film right before the big explosion, he throws his suit jacket over the couch, loosens his tie and the top button of his shirt to expose the soft pelt of chest hair I'd buried my face in with such relish back in Felicidad, and begins to fold his sleeves over the corded muscles of his forearms.

"Before the night is through, we're going to come to agree on how this thing between us is gonna go. Then I'll start installing the equipment meant to keep you alive."

"We spent one anonymous night together. There's nothing between us."

He pulls me into his body, his heat and cologne overwhelm my senses. "We'll address that comment later. For now, we need to establish a protocol that returns you home in one piece every day." Despite his brusque, business tone, his closeness wraps me in an intimate bubble; his breath fans my lashes.

I step away to clear my head. "Fine by me. Since you agreed to work with us, there's no reason for me not to follow your recommendations."

"Good, because if you deviate from my rules, don't blame me for punishing you. First, and most importantly, there will be no more solo bike rides until we get a handle on this situation." His green eyes darken to an almost black intensity.

Visions of his method of punishment are neither businesslike nor completely unwelcome. I rub my thighs together to quell the slickness seeping between them and begrudgingly nod my agreement in the ensuing silence. He seemed to require it before proceeding. He then goes on as if ticking items off a bulleted list, detailing all the check-ins and ways he will curtail my freedom. I have limited options and all his suggestions are reasonable.

But God does it chafe.

"I'm willing to discuss anything that requires a change in plans, but that requires open communication between us." He pauses as if waiting for an objection. When I don't, he says, "Now that we agree, I have to unload the equipment in the car. Is your house on a timed alarm?"

"No, but I'll lend a hand." I follow Lucien to his SUV hoping the activity will cool the slow fever developing under my skin. Stacked in the back two rows are countless hard utility cases. Some are lighter than others.

"If the need arises, I may supplement these with more equipment." He piles the cases in a corner off the entryway.

"All I ask is that you don't leave my walls looking like Swiss cheese."

"I'll do my best." He smiles and those cursed dimples make an appearance and undo my efforts to cool myself off. "The house suits you."

"What do you mean?" I glance around with fresh eyes.

Inside, I have a mixture of historical artifacts and modern designs that pay homage to music culture and the influences of many Black artists.

"It reminds me of the first time I saw you in that red dress. Your beauty sucker punched me first. Then your curiosity. It was obvious you'd never been to a club like that before, but you were open-minded, flexible… accepting. And then you sat beside me and I wanted to peel away the mysterious layers surrounding you, and now I'll get my chance."

"So my place is sexy and mysterious." I mull over his impression of me and nod. "I'll take it."

He sends me that lethal smile of his again, and I have to look away. "There is one thing I wondered about on the way here. Why didn't you move to the Garden District? Even without your father's money, I bet you can afford to live in the heart of the city."

"Who said I don't own property there?" I grin at his shocked expression. "I have several investment properties across the city, but I prefer living here. It's a nice mix that's close to my people, offers some security, and affords me the community feel I had growing up as a kid in West Lake Forest."

"I can tell how much that closeness means to you. While I ate your mama's food—which was amazing—I saw you joking around with your grandfather. The kind of warmth between you, heck all your family, told me you have a big heart."

There is a softness in Lucien's stare that tugs at the very organ he's admiring. Perhaps my reaction comes from the question I see behind his open green eyes, asking if there's room for one more. I don't have an answer for him. Having record-breaking sexual attraction is one thing, but this is altogether something else that I haven't planned for. He doesn't fit any of my expectations for the person who should monopolize my thoughts and emotions.

Lucien clears his throat, breaking me out of my thoughts. He clears his expression, and I almost miss the brief glimpse of his gentler side. I'm damned either way. Whether tender or domineering, I can't seem to stop myself from responding to him, to want to get closer to him.

"By the way, do you have to go into the office tomorrow?" he asks.

I desperately grasp at the new topic. "Why, do you think someone in my company has it out for me?"

"While I won't rule that out, no. It's too dark to do an effective install tonight."

"That's not a big problem. I can work from home. Before I turn in, let me give you a tour."

I show Lucien through the first-floor rooms. He pulls out the device he used at Cammy's. As he surveys the rooms, his gaze zooms in on all entry points, probably envisioning things like blind spots and other vulnerabilities. In each room, I wait until he indicates he has seen enough.

He retrieves his luggage, and I lead him upstairs to a guest room. I leave him to escape to my room, glad I didn't betray myself. But his gaze is a physical tether that doesn't loosen even after I close my bedroom door. I press my spine against the smooth wood grain, my heart beating fast as if I had run a marathon instead of walking a few feet away.

I make two calls to distract myself from the furnace raging inside my body. The discussions are short and in no way ease my current situation. There's no way I'll get to sleep without the aid of my O-makers tonight. Not with Lucien so temptingly close. I bet if he ever discovered I sleep nude, no protest would stop him from unleashing the domineering person he subjected me to in Felicidad. A steadying breath later and I head to the bathroom. Soon I'm struggling to keep my whimpering to a minimum as I work my vibrator on my clit, the memory of Lucien's voice pushing me harder and faster to a release.

I don't know how long I tend to myself, but with two or three fast and brutal self-induced orgasms under my belt, I walk to my vanity on wobbly legs, my nerves extra sensitive. I gently lotion my body, making sure not to overstimulate my nipples. Just as I turn down the covers on the bed, a knock at the door stills my hand.

"Can you open the door?" Lucien asks.

Shit!

Frantic, I rush to find something to cover myself. "Give me a sec," I call out. I glimpse the only robe I own, courtesy of my sister Thalie. As I attempt to close the garment, I realize the belt is somewhere still in my closet.

"Everything alright?"

"Be right there." I wrap the robe around me as best I can, hugging the material to my chest, and I crack the door open enough to see Lucien. When will I learn? I am never prepared to see him.

Water droplets glisten off his hair, lashes, and chest. I follow the trail of hair from his chest down to the waistband of his pajama bottoms. I can't deny my body's reaction to the outline of the monster I've had between my thighs, nor the reality of it coming to life the longer I stare. Abruptly, I raise my gaze to meet his and hug my chest tighter.

"It's about time we discuss that comment you made earlier," he says.

As much as I try, I can't for the life of me remember what he's talking about.

He pushes the door further ajar, and I instinctively step back. He stalks inside. "Since Sunday, I've been on a mission to find you. Now that I have, there's no way in hell I'm going to let that bullshit you were spewing earlier fly. There is something between us. I know you feel it every time we're in the same room. And when you come around to my way of thinking, you'll realize it's as permanent as permanent gets."

"You're insane."

"If I am, you're to blame, sweetheart. You stole all my reasoning the minute you walked out the door on me without a by-your-leave."

"That's pretty extreme. You—"

"Now look here, I wasn't alone in that club on Saturday. I know you felt this thing between us. It was a first for me and I understand that's probably what has you running scared. Ain't no shame in admitting you want more."

"Fine. I enjoyed myself. But it was just—"

"Do I have to remind you what I'll do if a lie leaves those pretty lips of yours?"

I clamp my mouth closed. The memory of his heated palm delivering a slap to my flesh undoes everything my session in the bathroom helped to alleviate.

"As I thought. I won't force you to say it, but understand that I already know and the feeling is beyond mutual. That's why we're going to switch up this living situation."

"Say what now?"

"Wherever you sleep, I'll be right next to you. The choice of which room is up to you."

"This is *my* goddamn house!"

Lucien continues as if I'd said nothing. "Tomorrow I'll have my medical records sent to you. I called my doctor yesterday in the hopes I would find you. Fate is obviously on my side."

At the mention of his medical records, an insidious thought feeds the growing inferno in my blood. I lick my lips and he zeros in on the action. "Why are you telling me this?"

"Because I want no barriers between us when we fuck."

Fuck. Me!

I gaze speechlessly at him. I almost don't recognize myself. I have never let a man twist me up this way, but I can't deny his pull. Despite his authoritative tone, on more than one occasion he's shown a willingness to listen that I rarely see in men at his level. I want to tell him to fuck off. To take the first plane back to Felicidad and forget my name. But Saturday night's memory continues to haunt me. What would it have been like without condoms?

I shake my head to dislodge the temptation. My hair slips over my shoulders, and I gather the individual twists in a ponytail and flip it over my right side.

A feral growl brings my eyes back to Lucien. Too late, I realize where he's staring. I forgot my arms were the only thing keeping my robe closed. I reach for the lapels, but with the lightning speed of a cottonmouth, Lucien grabs my arm and pulls me into his body.

"What exactly were you up to in here?" he asks. His grip is unbreakable but not painful.

A muscle ticks in his jaw, and I can't look away. The memory of his possessive claim on my pussy seals my lips. My silence only spurs him on. He surveys the bed that hasn't been touched and the nightstands. With only lamps as decoration, he loses interest in that area before he drags me into the bathroom.

He freezes at the threshold, inhaling deeply, his jaw clenching harder than earlier. I marvel at the pressure on display as he restrains himself while surveying the evidence showcasing my activities. On prominent display around my tub are my toys, still wet from their most recent cleaning.

"I don't understand what your problem—"

"How many times?" he grits as he tows me back into my bedroom. He quickly strips my robe from my body and pushes me onto the bed.

"Hey!" I leap up to wrest my robe back from his grasp.

"How many times?" he repeats.

I snap, "How many times what?"

"How many times did you stroke my pussy while I was down the hall? How many times did you make her come when you know it's my job to satisfy her? How many times did you suppress your screams because you knew I wouldn't take that shit lying down?" With each question he looms ever closer, his expression mildly containing the leonine hunter I likened him to at my daddy's house.

I push at his chest, and he stills. A heartbeat passes, and he disappears through my door, only to return in seconds. Not enough time to cover myself properly before he is once again stripping my robe from me.

"Tell me no. Right now. Tell me you don't want me," he says.

I open my mouth, but the words don't come.

He removes a foil package from his pocket. My eyes meet the determination in his. I can't deny the frisson of excitement along my spine. I know what's coming. In all truth, I want what's coming more than I want to celebrate Mardi Gras and Christmas every year. To know definitively that Saturday was not a fluke, that lightning can indeed strike twice. What little of my resistance that remains fades away under a new eagerness to revisit the overwhelming ecstasy only he has given me.

I remove the packet from Lucien's hold and rip it open with my teeth. His nostrils flare. I begin to bend, but he halts my progress and takes possession of the condom once again.

"You've been a bad girl, and bad girls have to work for their reward. Now, answer my question. How many times?"

The subtle threat in his words acts like a spigot, turning my weeping pussy into a flood of need.

"T-th-three, I think." God, why do I sound so hesitant? I'm a fucking boss. I run the streets in my territory. People know to fear and respect me. Yet here I am, weak-kneed over this golden country boy and eager to receive my punishment for my bad behavior. Bad behavior that shouldn't even count as I never agreed to anything beyond Saturday night.

Lucien drops his pajama bottoms, and all protests flee my mind. I lick my lips already envisioning burying my face in his freshly showered dick.

"Eyes up here, sweetheart." He waits for my compliance. "Once you've taken your punishment like a good girl, I'll grant you a reward."

My entire body shudders as the molasses-coated "good girl" leaves his lips. Heaven help me, I want to be his good girl. Always.

"Why don't you climb up on that bed and show me what I've been missing since Sunday morning," he says, throwing the condom still in the wrapper on the bed.

I rush to comply, uncaring that my ass jiggles as I move. His breathy intake tells me he approves. On my back, I spread my thighs.

"Spread those lips wider for me, sweetheart."

Although I follow his orders, his eyes don't travel to where my fingers splay my pussy for him. He ensnares me in his gaze as he bends down.

"Keep your eyes on mine. If you close them, you'll prolong your suffering." He inhales loudly. "You have no idea how I've longed for another taste," he says right before delivering a slow lick from the bottom of my pussy to my clit. At the top, he sucks in the tight bundle of nerves and lets it out with a loud plop and moan.

Oh, heavens above!

My hips strain to get closer to the devastation that is his mouth. He repeatedly licks me in this controlled manner and all I want to do is shove his face deep in my pussy and ride him for all I'm worth. More wetness seeps from me with every wet caress of his tongue and my body shudders at the overwhelming pleasure.

A stinging slap to my clit jolts me back into the moment. I stare wide-eyed and guilty as I recall his rule not to close my eyes. A hard glint enters his dark green gaze. It is my only warning before he plunges his finger inside my depths and engulfs my clit in his hot mouth.

There is no more teasing. He quickly finds my g-spot and relentlessly taps the muscle while he alternates flicking his tongue and sucking on my sensitive button. In no time, he ramps me up until I'm close to the edge, writhing and mewling and twisting the sheets in my fists. I'm desperate for him to push me over.

Then he stops. Bereft, I scream my frustration.

And Lucien? He stares at me while he wipes my essence from his face and licks his fingers clean. "Let's try this again. And this time, tell me every filthy need you have while I tend to my pussy."

"For how long?" I gasp.

"Until I forget your thievery." He plunges his devilish tongue inside me.

Although I follow his orders until I'm screaming nonsensical words, he does not let up. Over and over he brings me to the brink, his stare a lifeline keeping me tethered when I want to fly. But he never gives me that final push.

How would he react to knowing I pleasured myself on the days we weren't together? That the sound of his voice directing me became so unbearable I had to tend to myself over and over just to function? If this is how he retaliates for three orgasms, I wouldn't survive his methods for the ones I didn't keep track of.

The air is thick with my arousal and I desperately want to take a second to close my eyes and gather myself, but Lucien's warning prevents me from breaking contact. I've lost count of how many times he leaves me wanting and desperate. My thighs shake from holding my position for so long.

I probably look like a hot mess. Frustrated tears pour down my face as I beg him to give me what I need. He finally rises from his position on the floor and retrieves the condom he'd discarded earlier.

A desperate hope fills me as I lick my lips. Please, let this mean he intends to end my punishment and finally ease the empty ache in my pussy.

He leans over me, his elbows bracketing my head. For an eternity he holds my stare. Then slowly he dips his head and brushes his lips against mine. "I'm so proud of you, sweetheart. You sang your siren's song for me and I can't help but want to hear another number."

His words flood my body with pride and happiness. It doesn't matter that I haven't come yet. God, I only want to please him. I stroke his cheek and marvel at this new experience.

"You did so well for me, I think it's time you get what you've been begging for. Put me inside you."

Despite my eagerness, once I hold him in my hands, I can't stop myself from stroking his length. Lucien doesn't rush me. While I familiarize myself with his dick and cup his balls, he licks my lips until I open my mouth and accept the kiss I'd secretly dreamed about repeating since Saturday.

How could I have forgotten how we tasted together? I pull him closer for a deeper kiss at the same time I rest the crown of his dick at my entrance.

Lucien growls but makes no move to enter me. "If you want me to fuck you properly, you know what to do."

I raise my hips and pull his dick forward until the head enters my passage. In my ear, he repeatedly whispers that I'm his good girl and my body lights up and my heart thrums in happiness. It's more than the physical pleasure, although my body reactively shudders when he utters those words.

Two little words in the English language have never held so much power over me, yet they come with a sense of freedom I didn't know I was missing. The elation, the euphoria… they leave me speechless and open. They've unlocked a need inside me I suspect I'll no longer be able to live without.

Once Lucien is fully seated, he clasps our hands and brings them up to my ear. Like flipping a switch, the patient disciplinarian disappears, replaced by a raging mad beast of a lover. I don't know how he controlled himself until now, but he thrust his hips, pushing his dick further inside me. Powerful, deep, all-consuming. His lips are everywhere—my neck, my breasts, my ear. He licks, sucks, and whispers the filthiest, sexiest promises to me, and I can't wait for him to fulfill every last one of them.

It doesn't take long before he finally drives me into the most intense orgasm I've ever experienced. I can't fill my lungs with enough air to scream. My climax continues, one after the other because Lucien hasn't stopped fucking into me.

His thrusts lose their rhythm. He pumps as if desperate to reach every cell inside my body. "Zaïre," he roars as he comes.

As gruff and harsh as it is, it is still the sweetest sound I've heard from him. It's a sign that I'm not alone in this madness between us. That maybe he wasn't full of shit when he talked about permanence.

What am I thinking?

I try to shake free from this sex-induced euphoria. It has me imagining the impossible.

But is it impossible?

I quiet the voice inside my head trying to convince me this thing with Lucien will last beyond his assignment. He gets up and goes into my bathroom. He returns with a damp washcloth and gently cleans me. Even with the care he lends to the task, my body responds, and I moan.

"Ignore me. My body has a death wish," I say.

Lucien chuckles, his dimples and disheveled hair lending him a boyish look. He not only tucks me beneath the sheets, he ensures I'm on the dry side of the bed. He disappears but my eyes are too heavy to stay open while I wait for his return.

In the early hours of the morning, Tux jostles me. I'm used to this routine. He expects me to spoon him for the rest of the dark hours before I begin my workday. Without conscious thought, my body begins to roll over to accommodate my fur baby, but an arm clamps down on my waist and one on the back of my head. While I slept, Lucien transferred me onto his warm body, which is way more comfortable than it should be.

"You aren't trying to vanish on me again, are you, sweetheart?"

I peek at Lucien whose eyes haven't opened. "Not like I can get far. We're in my house. I was shifting because Tux wants to cuddle."

He peers down at the cat who gives him a baleful glare. "He'll have to find a new place to sleep."

"That's not how—"

"He's lucky I don't lock him out. He can either find a new toy to cuddle or he can leave. At night, cuddle-buddy rights to your body belong to me." Lucien ends the discussion with a squeeze to my waist and a kiss on my head.

He's in for a rude awakening. Tux does what Tux wants.

Yet the idea of Lucien holding me all night fills me with… comfort? Happiness? Yes, all the feels. And I realize the reason for my earlier restlessness was not having Lucien's possessive hold to look forward to. His arms shouldn't give me the same sense of homecoming that I usually get when I'm on my bike or when I return home from a stressful day, but they do.

I begin to drift off when Lucien's, "What the fuck?" jars me awake once more. Laughter bubbles out of me when I look up to find Tux curled above Lucien's head and his tail slapping Lucien in the face.

"Your cat is a petty little fucker, isn't he?"

"No one's ever dared to oust him from his territory. Here, let me get—"

"Stay where you are. Ain't nothing he can do to ruin this right here. He'll eventually accustom himself to the new arrangement." Lucien tilts his head, careful not to disturb the cat purring contentedly above him, and kisses my head.

Despite Lucien's tough talk, he's already making accommodations for my little guy. I snuggle into his hold and a smile sneaks onto my lips before I fall asleep for the rest of the night as visions of Lucien's new arrangement swim through my dreams.

CHAPTER SEVEN

Lucien

$\mathcal{M}$y internal alarm wakes me. With it comes a sense of peace I haven't had since before my army days. I hug the reason for my euphoric state closer. Zaïre's soft body is more of a home than the place I rest my head in Texas. This is the second time I've woken without thoughts of the men I've failed and the missions where I lost them. Missions I led.

I'm not unique. Many people in my shoes live with this type of survivor's guilt. Some adjust better than others. CESP, Connors Elite Security Professionals, is my way of channeling past regrets into something worthwhile. It's also a way to satisfy my thrill-seeking habit. Or maybe my habit came about because of all the shit I've been through. Either way, my company has made a name for itself and propelled me to the top of my industry.

My clients run the gamut from business execs, music moguls, alleged mafia enterprises, and even lesser-known royalty. But my most important client yet lies right here in my arms, and I vow she will have nothing to fear as long as I breathe. I soak in the moment for another few minutes before I gently disentangle our limbs. Tux seizes the opportunity to curl into Zaïre now that I am no longer molded to every inch of her body.

Downstairs I pair the Bluetooth speaker to my phone and raid her kitchen for coffee. I hit gold when I find a chicory blend. While the beans brew, I continue exploring until I gather ingredients for a decent breakfast. I lose myself to a country music station as I work. Nelly's "Lil Bit" begins to play and I dance while plating my and Zaïre's breakfasts. A quick shimmy and a spin later, I face a doubled over and laughing Zaïre. She becomes the target of my dance and serenade.

"Oh my God, please stop. You'll give me cramps from laughing so hard."

I grab her around the waist and rock with her, the flare from her skirt flirts with my legs. We stay in this embrace until she stops laughing and looks up at me with her shiny hazel eyes. Everything, and I mean everything that matters to me, is within her power to grant or destroy. Our future. Our happiness. And if I get all my wishes answered—and I pray to God I will—our future family stares hopefully at me right there in her golden-green irises.

We slow to a stop, never looking away from each other. The distance between us disappears and our lips meet. This kiss differs from the others. The frantic need is no longer present, but the meeting of our mouths is no less powerful. Maybe discovering Zaïre's identity is the reason. Knowing who she and her people are gives me a sense of security that calms the frenzy. We kiss until my lips are numb and we kiss some more. She buries her hands in my hair and I grip her hips tightly to me.

I slowly pull away, loving her swollen lips and dazed expression. "Good morning, sweetheart. Did my siren sleep well?"

She steps back and clears her throat. "Very well, thank you. Um, you know you didn't have to make breakfast." She makes her way to the kitchen island and sits in front of a place setting.

"How else am I going to make sure you eat properly before you start your day?"

Other than a shrug, she doesn't respond. This sudden display of shyness arouses my suspicion, but I try to let it go.

Halfway through her cheesy grits and eggs, she turns to me. "I'm sorry. I keep trying to understand what all this means and I'm drawing a blank."

"What all what means?"

"All this," she says, pointing to me, the food, and the kitchen. "All of a sudden you're Mr. Domesticity, calling me your siren. By the way, what does that even mean? And I can't help but wonder…"

"You think I'm putting on an act?"

She stares helplessly at me.

"For what purpose?"

"I don't know. That's what's driving me crazy."

"Just this once, I'll give you the benefit of the doubt. We still don't know everything about each other, so it makes sense that you have questions about me. I'm not the type of person who only looks out for myself. I need breakfast. You haven't eaten. Simple as that."

"And the siren thing? You called me that at my daddy's house."

"I did. Have you ever heard the legends about sirens?"

"Vaguely."

"Well, they are mythical creatures that were said to lure sailors to their death with the beauty of their songs."

"I'm a horrible singer."

"Not when you're coming you aren't. But that's not why you're *my* siren." I resume eating my breakfast and wait for the moment her curiosity gets the better of her.

She punches me on my shoulder. "Why am I *your* siren?"

I take her trembling hands in mine so she understands I'm not bullshitting. "Because I will follow you wherever you lead for the rest of my life."

Her eyes widen, and she licks her lips. "I…um…forgot… uh… I need to prepare for my first meeting. Thanks again for breakfast." Zaïre escapes, leaving half of her food uneaten.

I can almost see the smoke at her heels as she hauls ass to her office. I smile and shake my head. She will get used to my honesty and I can't fucking wait for the day she lowers her barriers and lets me all the way in.

She's teased me with her openness in bed, but my target is that big heart of hers.

≈≈≈≈

To make good on my early morning vow to protect Zaïre, I start the preliminary steps to connect her house to my corporate office's closed network system. Blake, Carter, and Darren will do the same for each Roudanez sister. The work is both physically and mentally absorbing.

I begin outside. The people after Zaïre are unknown entities with undetermined skills. I can't assume they're amateurs. To that effect, I install a combination of heat and motion detector cameras, all with night vision and a wide visual range so I can see who's coming before they realize they've been discovered.

Zaïre sets aside space in her home office for me to establish a surveillance hub where I connect each camera's recording. Try as I might to stay on task, Zaïre in her element as she teleconferences with her staff proves distracting.

"What's going on with Peters?" she directs her question to her executives on her computer screen.

Compassion resonates in her voice and it stops me from inspecting one last item before I check in with my team. For a woman in a male-dominated industry, some might mistake her as soft, but they would be blind. She is effective.

"We've stopped unloading the cargo for Price International but still haven't pieced together how the accident occurred. Since we're still within the twenty-four-hour window to report the incident to OSHA, I promise we'll get the details before they arrive for the investigation," a woman answers.

"That's all well and good, but I'm concerned about Peters right now. I heard his leg was crushed. What are we doing for him?" Zaïre's expression remains calm, but her tapping finger betrays a deeper emotion.

From my earlier eavesdropping, I imagine she is upset on this Peters' behalf. The more sneak peeks I get into her role as CEO of her shipping business, the more she impresses me. The more I admire her.

"Zaïre, as legal counsel I suggest we hold off on reaching out to him until we've gotten our story aligned. I'm meeting with our Human Resources and Public Relations departments later to minimize any fallout," a man's voice responds.

"Larry, I know you came here from a large corporation that may operate as if their employees are faceless individuals whose only purpose is to make profits for their execs. That's not how we work here. Peters is family and we will afford him the dignity he deserves. Right now, he's probably thinking about a million things that have nothing to do with us. The least we can do is offer him and his family some comfort. Now, what can we offer them while everything remains uncertain?"

She doesn't know this about me yet, but we are alike in this way. Instead of exploiting our employees for their labor, we genuinely care about their wellbeing. Heck, I bet she worries about anyone who depends on her like I do. And if that ain't the trait of a woman to admire, I don't know what is.

My instincts are rarely wrong, and witnessing her in action convinces me I was right to pursue Zaïre. She is more than a match for me. Although she tries to hide her soft heart, I've seen it in action with her family, that territorial beast she calls Tux, and now with an injured employee. I leave her to the rest of her meeting and open a group conference on my phone.

Leslie, my network expert, is the first to join. "Hey Enigma," he greets me with a mischievous grin. "You were the last to get me what I needed so it will take me another couple hours before I complete everything on my end."

"I swear if you call me by that name one more time, you'll find yourself in the unemployment line before you can say, 'What did I do?'"

"Duly noted," he says.

Like many others who've served as Delta operatives, I am tight-lipped about my service. All Leslie knows about my time in the military is from my pre-Delta career in the Army. Yet he continues to push to know more about the gap between my enlistment and discharge.

Blake, Darren, and Carter soon join the call. While I wait for one more person, Darren and I update the rest of the team about our secondary mission.

"Wait a minute." Leslie waves his arms, interrupting me before I get too detailed about what we need to do. "Are we protecting four assets, investigating a threat, and searching for that mystery woman from over the weekend?"

"No, the search is off. I found her and she's not going anywhere. There are only two directives this team is responsible for from now on." I pivot away from discussing my interest in Zaïre and outline what we'll need to do for the Roudanez family.

I don't care if my men know that I've crossed the line professionally with Zaïre. CESP is my company, and the only person I'm worried about finding out is Hammer, my actual client. They'll discover the truth when they meet her themselves. But for right now, our focus has to be on keeping her and her sisters safe.

"So, while we're reporting possible leads to the hub, will someone come to relieve you of your assignment?" Carter directs his question to me.

"No. Another team will be in charge of the groundwork."

The questioning glances on everyone's faces are understandable. If not for Zaïre, I would be leading the other team in rooting out the threat. She's also the reason for this special assignment since Hammer wants to handle things his way.

Shit, fighting danger's irresistible hum is a constant battle for me, but nothing is more important than safeguarding the woman who stole my heart with her feisty attitude.

"Who's gonna lead this new team then?" Blake asks.

As if only waiting for the question to be asked, Joel, the last member I'm waiting for, appears on the screen. A chorus of "ohs" erupts.

"Good to know I haven't lost my touch." Joel smirks at the screen. He is a cocky bastard with the skills to back up his confidence. Although I'll never admit it to his face, his capabilities far surpass my own. Luck must be on my side because he just came off his vacation in time for this assignment.

We coordinate our strategies and establish a daily check-in. If anyone is late, we'll escalate the situation and meet up at a safe house I purchased when Émile first reached out to me.

"Will your assets comply?" Leslie asks.

"Zaïre is on board."

"As is Jojo." Blake rubs his neck with a sheepish smile. "But I think it's thanks to Zaïre calling last night."

"Same for Thalie." Carter shakes his head with a similar expression to Blake. "On both counts."

Zaïre's endorsement is news to me, but I appreciate it. Although Camille is the eldest sister and president of their motorcycle club, Zaïre's word holds a lot of weight. I still remember our battle of wills at Émile's. The Roudanez sisters followed Zaïre's lead as if by instinct. Now with Zaïre removing roadblocks to their protection, there's one less complication in keeping the sisters alive.

"Camille may be a problem." Darren's revelation sours my hopeful mood. "Or more accurately, her *boyfriend*," Darren sneers. "He showed up last night and is on a campaign to convince her she doesn't need us. That my presence is a direct insult to his club and his standing as her man."

"Well convince her he's wrong," I say.

Having to confront Camille's relationship so soon after recognizing what she means to him must have sent Darren reeling. I'm not the type of man to let something like this fly when I know the woman is my destiny. Darren, as much as said he isn't either. But when the woman is as strong-willed as my Zaïre, staking his claim may backfire.

"Yeah, it's less about convincing her than it is him, but I'm not going anywhere. I said he may be a problem, not that I don't have a solution." Darren's firm jaw and fierce stare don't invite further questions.

I'll leave it alone for now because, like me, he will not jeopardize Camille's life over her relationship drama. Once we've discussed everything on my agenda and questions the team has, I ask Joel to call me for a one-on-one.

"I have a favor to ask," I say as soon as I answer the ring. I give him detailed instructions knowing he will come through for me. Once he agrees to everything, I try not to grin too hard as I await the joy on Zaïre's face when the surprise arrives.

Thinking of her reminds me of the late hour. Neither of us has eaten lunch. I reheat the leftovers in Zaïre's fridge and bring her a plate. At the door to her office, I take her in.

She hasn't noticed me. Her head is bent, her forehead puckered in concentration as she writes whatever amazing idea will further her success. Although I have no clue what she is writing, it must be something phenomenal to warrant that look on her face. She is fucking brilliant after all.

I shake my head to clear it of this fascination. It's not a temporary state, but one I'll savor when she can be a part of it with me. "You've been such a good girl, I thought I would reward you with lunch," I say.

Her body immediately shudders. She meets my stare with dilated eyes and her mouth opens on a silent gasp. Although not my intent, my mind immediately goes to giving her something worthy of her reaction.

"Um, Zaïre? Who is a good girl?" a deep voice says from her computer. A man's voice. A voice that sounds like competition, and I want to see who he is.

Zaïre's brown complexion darkens, making me all the more curious about the mystery man on the other side of her screen. I approach her, reminding myself not to revert to my raiding ancestors by claiming her on her desk for the other person to witness.

"Evan, have my admin reschedule this meeting for tomorrow morning when I'm on site." She clicks something in the middle of his response before she stands with her hands spread out on her desk, shooting fire from her eyes. "How dare you…I can't believe you would say that shit to me."

I place the plate of food in front of her. "I've been calling you a good girl since the first day we met."

Despite her locked stance, a small shudder betrays her and confirms my growing suspicion. "You like it when I call you a good girl. You sure as shit didn't react when that other guy said it."

"Please stop saying that," she says through another reaction.

"Why should I stop doing something that gives you pleasure?"

She storms over to me and pokes me in the chest. "Because I'm fucking working, you asshole. And what you just did could undermine me to my employee. How would you like someone showing up at your office in front of your team of macho men and making you react li—"

"You're right. What I did was wrong. I didn't realize you were in a meeting, and I let the casual setting override my common sense. I'll remember to confirm we're alone the next time."

"I-I…um…thank you?" She steps back, her head bowed and brow wrinkled in uncertainty.

"Sweetheart, were you expecting a fight?" I grin and stoop, trying to snag her attention.

"Ye—I mean you aren't the most accommodating person I know," she says as she raises her head.

"Now I take exception to that. I can be very accommodating. In fact"—I close the distance between us and lower my voice—"If you have free time right now I'll make up for my mistake."

Her breath catches. "What are you proposing?"

"Dealer's choice."

She glances at her computer, then faces me. "Anything I want?"

I quirk my eyebrow instead of answering. She licks her lips and grabs my hand. Curiosity rides my ass as she tows me up the stairs and into her bedroom.

"There is one thing you've stopped me from doing twice now."

Only one thing comes to mind. My cock hardens as the image of her on her knees pops into my head. I stopped her in the past because, as enticing as her mouth is, her pussy is the ultimate lure. I take my phone out of my pocket, set a timer, and show her the three minutes.

At her questioning glance, I say, "You have three minutes to make me come before I take over."

She has me throbbing and in her hand in seconds. "I do my best work under pressure." With a final squeeze, she lets go and pushes me onto the bed. "And don't even try to withhold your cum from me, lest I administer your punishment."

The chuckle I barely restrain bursts forth.

"You don't believe me?"

"I believe you'll do your best and I'll savor every second of your efforts."

Nothing Zaïre does could ever be considered punishment. Sweet torture, yes, but never punishment.

I raise myself on my elbows to the sight of her between my widespread legs. A determined gleam enters her eyes, a warning that my challenge won't go unanswered.

Before I completely forget myself, I press the start button on the timer and wait in delicious anticipation for what she has in store for me. My deviant little siren ignores my shaft and head, diving between my thighs to engulf my balls in her hot mouth. And, *oh fuck*, my mind blanks and my cock weeps in excitement.

I struggle to catch my breath, bathed in the sensation of

her smooth tongue performing the most excruciatingly delightful dance on my cock. I can't look away from her.

"You look so pretty sucking my cock."

"Mm moph."

"What's that sweetheart? You shouldn't talk with your mouth full."

Zaïre rises with a loud pop. "My cock," she says before swallowing me again.

I marvel at how much harder I get from her quick claim. When I do the same, does her body react as viscerally?

She is engrossed in tasting every inch of me, savoring me, and it is the hottest fucking thing I've ever experienced. I tense my muscles and twist the sheets in my fists. Shit, despite her warning, I do everything I can to fight off the coming explosion while her moans grow, and she sucks me in with the perfect amount of pressure.

On the brink of shooting what I expect will be a powerful stream, the alarm saves me by blaring its discordant tune.

"Time's up, sweetheart." I lift Zaïre and sit her in my lap and stretch the lacy barrier under her dress. My cock aches to be inside her. Her eyes glaze over with passion and her lips are swollen from being stretched. Like a lodestone her hand grasps my cock again, running it back and forth between her nether lips.

"Tell me now, do I pause this to get a condom, or do I give you the ultimate ride?" I made sure she not only received my test results but that she reviewed them on one of her breaks.

With a calculating smirk, she pushes me on my back once more. "This is still dealer's choice and I say sit back while *I* ride you." She thrusts herself on my cock and it's infinitely more pleasurable than anything I've ever felt in my life.

I am so lost in her softness I don't realize she has pinned my wrists to the bed. Not until she swivels her hips and my natural inclination is to take control of her body. I can easily overpower her, but I don't. Instead, I allow my sweet tormentor to torture me with each clench of her pussy, each press of her soft lips to my ear, neck, and mouth. I follow her, wanting the taste of her on my tongue which she denies me. My balls begin to tighten, and I realize she intends to send me on a solo trip.

Fuck that shit.

"Sweetheart, if you don't fuck me like you own me, you'll have played a losing hand and I'll have to remind you of all the ways I can make you sing."

Her motions stutter to a brief halt as if she needs to regroup her strategy. When she begins to bounce her juicy ass up and down, I assist with one aim in mind: to find the angle that sets her off like a rocket. I want to come so fucking bad, but not as much as I want her alongside me for the ride. A front-row seat to her cresting is a new discovery every time, an experience I will never tire of because her beauty while taken over by passion, rivals the most exquisite museum displays and all eight wonders of the world combined.

Her moans grow more desperate as does the rhythm of her hips. I increase my thrusts until she clamps down on me. I'm a fucking goner, but I'm not alone.

She screams, "Lucieeen!" until her voice cuts out.

I lose the battle to remain docile to her needs and hug her body close to me while I unleash a never-ending stream of cum into her. My mouth seeks another connection with hers. Once deprived, I now glut myself on everything she offers. It'll never be enough. My hunger for her is a bottomless pit and I never want it filled. I devour her lips and tongue and come back for more. Who needs fucking air when she can sustain me?

Her hand gently presses against my chest and I let her

pull away. "I have another meeting and I need to not look like I've been fucked halfway into next week."

I nod, although I don't want to. I much prefer making the appearance a reality or holding her until my arms go numb. But my siren wouldn't be who she is if she didn't take her responsibilities seriously. And she definitely wouldn't have a stranglehold on my heart if she were that fickle.

"I think it'll be better if I'm not in the office until your day is done. Then I'll walk you through the new security measures I installed." I survey her wrinkled dress. I almost regret not taking the time to take it off her.

"That's probably a good idea. I'll just wash up first."

I grab her wrist before she can get too far. "Only your face. Keep my cum inside you until I can clean you properly." I slip out of her and adjust her panties.

"Lord Jesus, the mouth on you…"

"Is the same one that'll make you come hard again tonight." I smile when instead of heading to the bathroom, she grabs a few items from her vanity and makes a hasty escape to her office.

I clean myself and head to the door only to find Tux barring my way. We size each other up. Tux, I discovered, has a weakness I'm not beyond exploiting. I bend down and let him get acquainted with my scent. He closes the gap between us immediately, and I realize it's thanks to Zaïre's essence on my clothes. I rub the thin skin of his ear, and the territorial monster turns into the purring pussycat he was meant to be and closes his eyes in ecstasy. With some added praise, I unlock the magic key to his loyalty. Just like his owner, although she hasn't admitted it yet. To me or herself.

But she will.

CHAPTER EIGHT

Zaïre

*I*t has only been a week, yet Lucien occupies all the empty spaces in my house. And if I'm honest, my mind as well. And it's not just all the fucking we do, though I'm amazed I haven't gotten a UTI or started walking bowlegged. Even Tux, the little traitor, has become an equal opportunity cuddler, switching between Lucien and me as if we are interchangeable.

I don't know how he broke my cat and I'm not completely sure if I'm mad, sad, or disappointed.

What I need is a ride. I've never gone this many days without getting on my machine and taking off on the high-way. It's not that Lucien has me trapped in a boring routine. As long as I inform him where I want to go, he makes a plan to accommodate me. I just find sitting in the back of his luxury armored tank that passes for an SUV to be a stifling experience.

And I absolutely do not want to show up to our Flossers meeting tonight in an SUV when everyone will have their specialized wheels on display. I search for Lucien and find him in the backyard fiddling with one of the motion sensors he installed last week.

"There a problem?" I ask.

"Not sure. The signal from this unit disappeared and I'm checking for signs of tampering." He replaces the sensor and stands. "I'll need to check the other cameras to rule out if it malfunctioned due to manmade interference or nature."

I still haven't gotten used to his overwhelming appeal or his insistence on making me his focus. Too many times I look for the hint of amusement never far from the surface just so I can peep his dimples. I swear they do something to my heart…and other areas. But now, as I look around my neighborhood, I wonder about Lucien's comment about a person sabotaging the equipment.

He checks the cameras and heads inside to his NSA-level setup. We watch the footage from last night into the morning but nothing detectable shows up. I sigh in relief that someone hasn't gotten so close to me without us knowing, but it is a reminder that I can't rely on Lucien and his team alone. I have to practice vigilance myself.

"It's a good thing nothing showed up," Lucien says, facing me with a knowing smile. "I have a surprise for you. I've been waiting for days and it finally arrived."

I'm immediately suspicious. Not because I won't like whatever he may have in mind. He hasn't disappointed me yet. But the guard didn't notify me about a special delivery. Then again, I'm not surprised. Lucien made a point of intro-ducing himself as my private security, and the men have been buddy-buddy ever since.

No, my caution stems from whenever that smile appears and Lucien pimps out his dimples. When they make an appearance, there's a fifty-fifty chance I'll end up with him inside me and I cannot show up to a Flossers meeting looking like I've been fucked to India and back. Not when we have serious shit to talk about tonight.

Lucien takes my hand and leads me to the front of the house where there is a well-maintained Kawasaki H2 motorcycle sitting prettily in my driveway. I arch my brow in question.

"Joel finally had time to drop off my baby. I had a feeling you would tolerate the SUV for only so long and I wanted to share this with you."

"You ride?" I circle the bike with more enthusiasm. "How are you only telling me this now? Oh, yeah, it was a surprise. But...I thought you objected to me riding my bike before."

"Because you're a fucking speed demon and an SUV can't keep up with the way you weave through cars. And since we're on the subject of your safety, I have a few maneuvers and formations we need to walk through before we leave."

He details the different ways he intends to protect my back, side, and front depending on what either of us sees, hammering home that I have to communicate with him through agreed-upon signals anytime I sense if anything is off.

"I don't care if it's a fly in the corner of your eye. You sense something, you signal me, and I'll get you to safety. I've already mapped a few alternate routes."

"Okay, I'll do all that. Can we get on the road now?" Energy pulses through me and I bounce from one foot to the other.

"Yeah. Go get your bike." His smile is full of warmth and indulgence.

"Thank you, Lucien."

The next thing I see is Lucien's surprised face when I throw myself into his arms and kiss the living shit out of him. Before long, his reaction turns to a sinful chuckle, and he takes over the embrace to steal my breath from my very lungs.

We separate, panting heavily with our lips almost touching as if the temptation to indulge in just one more wouldn't make me late and have Cammy riding my ass about the reason.

"It's a shame I can't surprise you since you're on the job all the time." I caress his cheek, our gazes locked onto each other.

"Give me a date and I'll make whatever surprise you want to give me happen," he says with a final innocent peck on my eyelid.

For the entire ride, it isn't the hot, steamy kiss that preoccupies me but the feel of his soft lips on my eye that continues to spread warmth inside me while wind buffets my body. This time with Lucien, devoid of speech as we perform an otherworldly dance, beautiful in its unrehearsed choreography, is the most freeing time I've ever spent with a man. I want to capture this moment and mold it in bronze forever. More than once I have to remind myself to be on the lookout.

We exit the highway and drive towards the port, the scent a mixture of industrial and marine waste. It's all shit and overpowering and the opposite of anything anyone wants to smell, but it's familiar.

Warehouse workers and fishers line the sidewalks as they go about wrapping up their day. As the population thins, the hair on my neck shivers with tension. The people here don't have the industrial air about them. Their eyes are desperate, mercenary; willing to sell their kid for any amount of money.

One particular set appears, then disappears when I glance in their direction. An uneasy chill skates down my back. I signal to Lucien and he inserts himself between me and the sidewalk, dampening the effect from the stranger.

We ride straight onto my company's property to a warehouse I had converted specifically for our meetings. Daddy calls his get-togethers church, but we ladies like to put a different spin on the patriarchy. We are here for Tea.

The debutants arrive first. They aren't patched members yet, but they ride in proud, loud, and burning. These moments before the meeting starts are always a fashion show of sorts. Our members dress in designer outfits paired with couture heels from independent to established fashion brands. Amid the colorful smoke from their spinning wheels, they show off their rides and techniques to the encouraging catcalls of fellow Flossers.

Soon after, the warehouse fills with member chatter and the lingering exhaust from outside. Lucien and his men stand in the back of the warehouse attracting curious glances from our members.

Although surrounded by gray, heavy machinery and boxy buildings, the inside is fit for our stylish riders. Amidst the elegant furnishings, there is a bar, a section for our nail salon technician, a lounge area, and our pop-up merchandise shop for our branded goods. I catch Lucien and his team gaping at the unexpected combination.

This is the first Flossers meeting since my sisters and I learned about the threat to the club a week ago. It took Joel that long to investigate and clear every member, which came as a relief because we have a lot of updates to share.

Our broker, Owl, calls the roll. When putting in an appearance at her family's weekly dinner, she goes by Minh but Owl fits her better, her knowledge is endless.

Camille begins the meeting with old business. When it gets around to new business, I update everyone on the new Oliveri deal, and Brinks, our treasurer, congratulates us on another successful quarter with an increase in protection funds coming through.

The news surprises me as folks in the ninth ward are soliciting us for protection instead of the other way around. We won't accept, of course. That's Bayou Hellraiser territory, and one stipulation we agreed to is to keep a healthy gap between our terrain. We've kept to our word and although Daddy retired, he still holds a lot of sway. No one in his club would dare to harm us for fear of his retribution. But in the back of my mind, I can't deny the whisper questioning if this is the cause behind the ambiguous threat.

I shake the thought from my mind and tune into our enforcer Stealth as she details the threat we're facing, yet the insidious thought creeps in when I least expect it. Stealth's real name is Cantrelle but Stealth fits her better, and not just because she is the fastest rider we have. She can find anyone no matter what obscure hiding place they've found, faster than the government tracking a Black activist. Once we know who we're dealing with, we'll be in a race to get to them first. As much confidence as I have in Lucien's team, I'm betting everything on Stealth.

"Flossers," Cammy says, "whatever you do, repeat nothing to no one outside of the people in this room. Report anything suspicions to our officers. And debutants, while we're still ignorant about who wants to harm us, don't look at this as an opportunity to get your patch. You'll find plenty of other dangerous opportunities ahead of you."

The ladies murmur amongst themselves. We open the floor for discussion and end the meeting with our Chaperone, Tamika, confirming the date and location of our next run to Bourbon, Texas. It will be an important event as Daddy's Bayou Hellraisers will add to our numbers. Because of the potential security breach, the Hellraisers believe our final destination is two towns over. Unbeknownst to them, they'll also provide extra coverage most of the way as this trip marks the Flossers' first shipment of weapons under our contract with the Oliveris.

The members leave more sober than they arrived, probably hearing Cammy's warning on repeat in their heads. Alone but for our bodyguards, my sisters and I reconvene in the back office and the men station themselves at strategic points outside the room.

"I feel like it's been ages since we went on a bike run. I can't imagine how Cammy has held up all this time." Thalie stretches her arms behind her head, then plops onto the couch.

I turn to Cammy realizing the usual excitement at the prospect of a run is nowhere to be seen. "How have you held up? It's been a minute since you and Smoke rode together. I thought you'd be hassling us to solidify all the planning for the trip at least every five minutes."

Cammy shrugs. "I don't know. Smoke has been acting kinda funny lately and it's taking the joy out riding to Bourbon."

Jojo sidles up behind Cammy and hugs her. "Not to mention we haven't made much progress on who's after us. Daddy ain't budging on giving us clues. I even tried the baby daughter act that he *always* falls for and I got nothing. I can't help but think it's more serious than we expected."

"Have any of you seen anything suspicious over the last week or on your way here tonight?" I ask.

"I wouldn't say I saw anything suspicious…" Thalie trailed off, a wrinkle in her brow.

"But?" Cammy asks.

"It was more a sensation that something was off. It happened soon after I got off the highway but a good distance from here so I ignored it."

"Something like that happened with me too." Cammy

folds her arms. "Take a different route on your way home tonight. When everyone gets home, we'll do a group chat and check in. And Thalie, next time you sense anything is off, tell Carter. We can't afford to keep things to ourselves."

"This is new coming from you," Jojo says.

"Maybe, but I'm not liking this new feeling."

Neither do I.

CHAPTER NINE

Zaïre

"I still can't believe you flew another bodyguard here all because I wanted to surprise you." I look over to Lucien who, unexpectedly, hasn't complained once about the blindfold over his eyes. We are in the back of the SUV—a first for us—while Marcus, our guard for the day, takes over protection duties.

Lucien stretches his hand in my direction until he meets the flesh of my arm. He pulls me into his side and wraps his arm around my waist with a satisfied sigh. "I delight in giving you things you like. Plus, when you told me blindfolds were involved, I had an altogether different image in my head, which I plan to make a reality at some point."

I melt into him. I do that a lot. It should grate on my last nerve, and it does until he melts into me, too, which is something he is beginning to do more often. And with no prodding or ordering on my part. It has to go against everything he is as a take-charge decision-making boss but there's an added quality in his embrace and the kiss to my eye that tells me he gets more out of it than he or I expected. And every time he softens, I have to silence my inner squee because I'm a grown-ass woman.

"Yes, you are, sweetheart. And I can't wait to rub on that grown ass some more tonight."

How did I not hear the words come out of my mouth in time to gag them too? "Lord Jesus."

"You can pray all you want. Preferably kneeling and with your mouth full of my cock. Ooh." Lucien shakes his head with a heated glance that puts my body on high alert. "Once I get you alone, best you believe the only prayers getting answered will be mine." Lucien acts as if he doesn't know damn well that Marcus can hear everything he says.

Yep, that grin playing at the corners of Marcus' mouth tells me he heard every bit of my exchange with Lucien. If I try to pull away, it will be useless. Lucien will not let me loose and I don't really want to be free. We drive for a few miles before Lucien shifts restlessly.

"Sweetheart, your surprise don't have nothing to do with the Bayou, does it? Not saying I won't enjoy it. With you by my side ain't nothing I won't find pleasing. I'm just hoping I'll have the opportunity to linger over my favorite sights." Lucien trails his hand up my inner thigh only to stop a breath away from my pulsing clit, my panties a nonexistent barrier to what my pussy wants.

I clear my throat but it's no good. Images of Tux riding on my bike flash before my eyes, his cuteness and attitude dampen the passion Lucien's touch ignites enough for me to rasp, "Boy, I am a citified Negro. I may enjoy what the Bayou provides, but I do not, and I cannot put enough emphasis on this, *enter* the actual Bayou. Just because I'll eat a gator don't mean I need to go into their habitat for tea."

"Then tell me where you're carrying me off to." His finger caresses my outer labia, and he smiles at the first contact of the damp fabric against my folds.

Lucien's effect wears me down, and I no longer care about Marcus as I straddle Lucien's hips and devour that filthy mouth of his while rubbing against his hardening length. His taste is sin and unfulfilled temptation wrapped together, and I can never get enough of him.

How will I deal when he's gone?

I shake the thought from my mind, nowhere near equipped to handle all the emotional baggage his job presents, but determined to enjoy him and this situation while it lasts. I kiss him harder, nipping his bottom lip, knowing he won't let me control our kiss for much longer.

Without dislodging our lips, he flips and presses me into the seat. My mind splinters into a colorful kaleidoscope. It's exactly what I need from him and he delivers. I moan into his mouth and he slips two fingers past the edge of my panties to enter me in one quick thrust.

My hips act on their own, pressing into him and urging him to give me more. More pressure. More depth. More him.

"That's right, sweetheart. Ride my hand like the good girl you are," Lucien whispers before taking my mouth in another heated kiss.

Tension builds inside me, and the edge is so close I can almost touch it.

Then the motherfucker stops mid-stroke.

I break away from the kiss to lambast him to hell seven times over only to realize the car is no longer in motion and Marcus is standing by my open door.

"I really hate you for leaving me this way," I say.

Lucien licks his fingers and my body thrums to the rhythm of his groans. "Sweetheart, we're in the same boat here. Unless you want an audience?" He nods toward the draft from the open door and to Marcus who surveys the area with a determined air.

"No, that's not my style."

His nostrils flare and his mouth firms. I'm reminded of our first night together when he took everything I said as a challenge and proved all my misconceptions wrong. My pussy clenches and my nipples tighten. Do I want him to fuck me with an audience?

"I can get on board with that." Lucien smiles and sets those devilish dimples free. "For today, the only person who needs to hear you purr is me."

To change the subject and allow my body to cool, I say, "Since we've arrived, you can take your blindfold off."

Lucien pushes the fabric off his head and a momentary frown of confusion crosses his face. I wait for the moment he connects the dots.

"Are you taking me on a helicopter tour?"

"Not quite." I lead him inside where a man greets us with paperwork.

"Are you shitting me?" Lucien asks as he reads through the documents. Another smile blossoms on his face devoid of mischief but strong enough to power cities. And those dimples get me every time.

I respond more slowly, reeling from the impact of his joy. "The other night you mentioned you had a license but never got enough air time."

He wraps his arm around my waist and pulls me into his side. In my ear he growls, "Sweetheart, you know this qualifies as good girl behavior, right?"

I shiver at both the raspy quality of his voice and what being his good girl means. I don't have a Daddy kink, but whenever Lucien uses those approving words my body glows from the inside and readies itself in anticipation of my reward. Because of our arrival, I didn't get the reward his words promised. But he's now said good girl again, and the effect so soon after he left me wanting in the car only serves to bring me on the brink again. If he touches me now, even if only to kiss my eyes closed, I might embarrass myself, and his earlier act of discretion will have been for nothing.

I lean into him so no one can hear me. "Just so we're on the same page, I get two rewards." I hold up two fingers to emphasize my seriousness.

Lucien brings my fingers to his lips. "Sure, sweetheart. And for one of them, I might even let you choose the reward."

The employee leads us through a different exit where another staff member stands by the open door of a helicopter. Lucien and I board, put on our headphones, and moments later we are in the air overlooking New Orleans. I can't keep my eyes off him. His command of the aircraft and its myriad of controls reminds me of his mastery in other aspects of his life, including me.

The headphone speakers guarantee that I hear Lucien despite canceling out the noise in the cabin. "Did you fly in the army?"

He glances at me. "No, but I made friends with a few Night Stalkers, the special ops army pilots. They convinced me I would love the thrill. After my discharge, I had a hard time dealing with life as a civilian and remembering the people I lost on my missions. It got so bad there were many days I never left my house unless it was to restock my booze. Thanks to my family, especially Darren who refused to let me wallow, I got my ass up, forced myself to look in the mirror, and decided to do something that would honor the men I lost in the field. That's why I filled my time with building my business and getting my pilot's license. Again, with a ton of support from my family. Long story for a simple question, I know."

"I'm glad you told me."

"Sweetheart, there ain't nothing I wouldn't tell you." He winks at me and turns back to the scenery in front of us.

"If not for the favor you owe my daddy, would you still be in Texas overseeing the business?"

"Not sure. I like to be close to danger so I might have accepted another job doing something like Joel is doing for us. Would have been a damn travesty if fate hadn't intervened and brought us together again."

This is the second time he's referenced us and fate in the same sentence, and a strong urge to revisit my religion and become a believer comes over me. Because believing in fate means believing in permanence, in the future. It also means believing in Lucien. And I desperately want whatever he sees when he looks at me with those clear green eyes of his.

" Then again, I'd like to think I would have ended up in New Orleans eventually."

"Why's that?"

Lucien glances at me. "I was ready to lose one of my biggest clients by hacking his system because he refused to give me your name. And before I saw you in Hammer's living room, I already had a team dedicated to tracking you down. And you know once I discovered who you were, there wasn't nothing that could stand in the way of me finding you."

I take a deep breath to process what he's told me. It's everything I want to hear, but cannot embrace while thousands of feet in the air. To give myself time, I clear my throat and ask, "Are you using the danger to compensate for something?"

"Why? You worried for me, sweetheart?"

I am, but I'm not stupid enough to use it to stop him from doing what he loves. Although I suspect he would stay behind a desk if I asked. "I wouldn't try to stop you if that's what you're asking. Signing that NDA didn't make you deaf.

You know I do more than own a cargo company. I wake up every day with danger breathing down my neck. Sometimes I make her my bitch and put her to work for me. Sometimes I need a professional to keep me safe." I rub my hand down his arm, relishing in his flexing muscles.

"Well, to answer your question, I don't know. It might be a combination of me taking someone's place so I don't lose another man and my thirst for excitement." He turns to bore his gaze into mine. "I've been thinking about it these past few days because when I'm with you, you quench all my thirsts. I imagine you doing so for all my lifetimes to come."

My heart sputters to a standstill before racing out of my chest for the next country.

How does he keep doing this to me?

"I…um…think it's nice your family supports you whenever you need it." I break our eye contact and look out of my side window. Why can't I be normal and give him the cheesy response he deserves when I want to grab onto the vision he paints with a stranglehold?

Lucien allows the change in subject. I peek at him over my shoulder but nothing in his demeanor tells me if my deflection bothers him. "Your parents must support you, too. Words of praise, showing up, money? Otherwise, your Flossers would have met with way more obstacles in getting established."

"That was more from my granddaddy's influence. He knows how to get under Daddy's skin like none other, especially if he uses my mother's name in an argument. Otherwise 'The Hammer' would have had us all boo'd up with one of his Hellraisers. As for praise, he considers everything we do as hobbies that take our time away from more important *womanly* duties. It would hit softer if Mama outright checked him, but she tells us, 'he don't mean nothing by it' and we all gotta swallow our pride because he's still our daddy."

"Hmm."

"What?" I glance over at him but he's concentrating on our descent. "Is it time for us to return already? And I took up all your airtime yammering in your ear."

"Isn't this a date?"

"Yes, but—"

"Dates are for getting to know each other better. That's what we did. Besides, anytime you're by my side is worthwhile. The flying is a bonus I never expected."

We land and meet up with Marcus who takes us to our next stop, my favorite restaurant. Lucien is quiet the entire ride. I'm not given time to worry that I said something to upset him because he holds me in his lap and strokes my back until I lose all tension and I rest my head under his chin. We continue to get to know each other over dinner but I can't ignore the voice inside my head telling me all isn't right with him.

He silences the doubts whispering in my ear with a blistering kiss the moment we walk through my front door. Smoky bourbon from his last drink and Lucien's natural flavor overwhelm my senses. I scratch at his clothes wanting him naked. Now!

Fabric rending is my only warning before he hauls me up and impales me against the door. I wrap my legs around his hips for purchase.

Lucien doesn't give me time to breathe, to think, not even to scream before he snatches my breath with his punishing thrusts. The door rattles under the onslaught. I pray the neighbors don't call the police thinking I have a violent intruder. I mean, I do. But Lucien is the best kind of intruder a girl can ask for.

I should probably feel pain between his forceful pumping and the hard door on my spine, but I am so wet and wanting. The only thing splintering my mind is the immense pleasure that only Lucien can deliver. I try to rip open his clothes to get access to his warm skin, but he captures my wrists and holds them prisoner above my head.

"Not this time, sweetheart. This is the reward you earned tonight, and you'll take what I give."

"Dammit, Lucien. I need to touch you."

"We are touching, sweetheart," he says then proceeds to slam into me again and again while biting down on my neck and driving me wild as he massages my clit with his free hand. "Don't you feel how my pussy is caressing my dick? Touching me all over? How happy she is that I'm ending her wait?"

I fight to get closer to him, but I'm no match for him when he is determined to fuck me into oblivion. The moment I surrender I orgasm. Hard.

He presses his head into my shoulder and stops moving his hips. His hard dick pulses inside me and although full, I feel cheated that he sent me off on my own. I pull at my hands. Instead of releasing me, he brings his green gaze hazy with lust to mine.

"You didn't come."

His cheek throbs and he sharply inhales. I realize he doesn't intend to answer me, and I begin to question how long he intends to stay inside me when he pulls out and presses me to the floor.

"Tonight, you will get many rewards, not just the two you asked for," he says to my upturned face. He guides his dick to my lips, and I take him in hungrily. He holds my nape and controls how much of his length I suck and lick. But he can't control my enthusiasm. His body tenses and he groans his satisfaction.

I love Lucien's dick, especially when it is coated in my cum. Almost as much as I love Lucien. My body stills.

"What's the matter, sweetheart?" he asks me.

I mumble, "Nuffing" with my mouth still full and try to clear any shock from my face.

He hisses as I diligently reapply my efforts. With my hands free I grab his ass and pull him into my face, for the moment taking him by surprise. I allow my greedy need for Lucien to overtake me, and it must have worked.

"Fuck, siren. Not yet."

I ignore him. He's too late, anyway. Spurt after spurt of cum sprays my throat and I swallow, unwilling to waste a single drop. He pulls me up by my neck and I stare at him unrepentantly.

"I decided to take *my* reward all at once," I say.

"You think I'm so stingy there ain't more where that came from?" He doesn't give me a chance to respond. As if I'm not a plus-sized woman with a big ass, he bends me over his shoulder and takes me upstairs to my bedroom, displacing Tux, and begins to "reward" me for the rest of the night.

In the early morning hours, wrung out and overly sensitive to touch, I peer into Lucien's eyes. Emotions I've never experienced have a stranglehold on my throat. As if sensing the maelstrom beneath my surface, Lucien gently embraces me. He lays soft kisses along my body and caresses me until a sweet orgasm sweeps over me. It is all the more powerful because throughout it all we never break eye contact, and the intensity almost brings me to tears.

Through all the sweaty hours and countless orgasms, it is the last one that weakens me. I am amazed I have the wherewithal not to blurt out my inconvenient discovery because no matter what sweet words Lucien utters, he has never mentioned what permanence between us looks like. No questions about me moving to Texas or him to Louisiana.

I reach for him, desperate to hold onto him while I can.

"Something wrong, sweetheart?" Lucien kisses my forehead.

I bury my face into his neck to avoid his perceptive gaze. "No, I just want to hold you until I fall asleep." I breathe him in, memorizing our combined scent.

"Well alright. You just about guaranteed my dreams will be the sweetest." Lucien tightens his arms around me.

I silence the sob growing in my throat at the future ahead. He will leave, and I refuse to foist my feelings onto him before he does. If I keep them to myself, on the fateful day Lucien departs for his next assignment, only I will have to live knowing that he will take my heart with him.

CHAPTER TEN

Lucien

*I*f I had any doubts about my feelings for Zaïre, watching her interrogate the lead Joel's team identified would have settled the matter. Despite the oddness that being surrounded by an air of suppressed violence brings, my chest fills with a warm fire.

But I never doubted that Zaïre was the woman for me, so our location is unimportant. What starts a low thrumming in my chest are the hints that she is finally accepting this love growing between us. She took me on a fucking date. Not just any date. One tailored to a random comment I made about something I never find enough time to enjoy.

Because she listens. Because she fucking cares.

Fuck, my heart is bopping back-to-back dances of the one-step, the shuffle, and the two-step.

"Tell me who is behind the threats to my family," Zaïre

says. "We don't have history, so someone is pulling your strings."

We're in the basement crematorium of a funeral home Owl owns under the Flossers' holding company. It's still early in the morning, but Zaïre received a call from Camille, delegating the questioning of Joel's find to her. I get the impression Camille is playing peacekeeper between my brother and Smoke. I haven't met the dude, and my bias puts me on Darren's corner, but I've heard enough about him from Zaïre and I don't get his appeal.

Tied to an embalming table over the tarp-covered floor in the stark concrete setting is a redheaded man. Various embalming implements have been inserted into his body to drain and inject him with fluids. The setup makes him appear like a macabre experiment. His nose and mouth are bloody, consequences from not answering Zaïre's questions.

"Little girls who play at being in the mafia don't scare me," the cocksucker says.

He must not value his life. I curb the impulse to intervene because if I get involved, I can't say I would have enough control not to rip out the asshole's tongue and force-feed it to him. Besides, Zaïre can handle herself. I could never be this gone over a weak woman.

"We're having a friendly conversation here. Ain't no need to disparage nobody." Zaïre sits and crosses her legs in an armchair Stealth brings to her. Zaïre is sexy as fuck in a red power pantsuit and heels that complement her dark brown complexion.

I wonder if she chose that color to remind me of our first night together. If so, she's succeeded. I work twice as hard not to envision the way she looked that night and everything we did so I can concentrate on my job.

And right now my job requires me to watch over her while she questions Billy. He's the man Joel picked out after watching countless surveillance feeds of the Roudenaz sisters' workplaces. Although he only had grainy photos to go on, Joel identified Billy quickly. But our quarry disappeared with little for us to go on. Zaïre overheard my call with Joel and convinced me to share the intel.

That was last night. Stealth called Camile this morning with the news she'd found him. Camille told her to hold him until Zaïre arrived. I would poach Cantrell for my company if it wouldn't mean leaving Zaïre without a fierce protector, not to mention sacrificing my balls to Zaïre's anger.

"Now, Billy. Since I'm a little girl who can't understand anything, why don't you explain yourself? Why were you sneaking around my company?"

"You're smoking crack, bitch. I wasn't anywhere near your piece of shit company."

"I have you on camera. And my colleague found these items on you." Zaïre points to a table holding a small bottle of chloroform, a cloth, and a Glock. "What do you need these for?"

At his continued silence Zaïre nods. "Let me explain what will happen to you since you haven't grasped the precarious position you're currently in. That"—she points to a pink fluid in a machine connected to Billy—"is a one percent formaldehyde solution. The longer you hold out on me, the more I'll up the concentration."

Billy glances between the machine and Zaïre. Doubt flashes across his face, then disappears.

"Do you know what happens when a live person gets injected with embalming fluid, Billy?"

"Fuck you."

"Your blood feels like it's boiling from the inside, as though I'm pouring acid directly into your body. You'll experience slight discomfort at first. Then each time I up the dosage, the more painful it becomes. But if you tell me what I want to know soon enough, you might walk out of here alive before your body succumbs to convulsions and your organs begin to shut down. Don't say I didn't warn you."

The door behind me opens. With one glance, I assess the situation and intercept the man bulldozing his way to his daughter. "Hammer, don't interrupt what's happening here." I take his elbow and retreat to a corner to keep our conversation from distracting Zaïre's work.

He pulls for me to release him. "You need to explain yourself right motherfucking now, you heard me. I've been looking for that asshole." He struggles to twist left and right but his efforts are useless against my grip.

"Keep your voice down!" My harsh response causes him to pause.

He glares at me and through a clenched jaw, he says, "Explain yourself."

"How'd you know she was here?"

After a few seconds of a standoff, complete with fierce staring, Hammer relaxes. "One of my guys saw Stealth sniffing around his place last night. When no one saw him today, it took little effort to guess who was behind his disappearance. And why the hell are you way over here? How you supposed to stop a bullet when there's a goddamn country of space separating you?"

"Now, Hammer. We've known each other for a good while. You know I take my work seriously. But you need to open your eyes."

"What're you saying?"

"Stop treating your daughter like she's still on your knee begging for sweets. Not only is she an adult, she's successful and accomplishes what she sets out to do. And right now she's working."

"She got to you, didn't she?"

"If you're asking if I'm in love with her, that should be

clear. And even more reason for you to believe I will always put myself between her and any bullet coming at her."

"Yet you're over here shooting the shit while she…while she…I never wanted this life for her or any of my girls." His shoulders slump.

I no longer sense the combative air he marched in here with, so I release him.

"I know that might not make any sense since I always had them around my Hellraisers. Showed them off like they were trophies. Can you blame me? Ain't nobody got girls as smart and pretty as mine. Why wouldn't I show them off? And you can call me foolish if you want because, after all that, the most involved I ever expected them to be was as someone's Old Lady. That way they'd benefit from our protection, but never be in the line of fire, you heard me."

"I understand your concerns, but she chose this life. You didn't push her into it. She went to college. Twice. She owns a male-dominated business. She knows her mind, and you need to take a good look at her now, Hammer. Zaïre is the danger here. And she's a goddamn goddess at work."

Billy's scream punctuates the point I make to Émile. We glance at Zaïre to watch as she injects the first round of fluid into her captive. Billy thrashes and gnashes his teeth between bouts of shrieking.

"I never knew she had it in her," Émile whispers, eyes widening as if seeing his daughter for the first time.

"If you stop underestimating her, you'll discover there's a lot more to your daughter than someone who needs coddling." I fold my arms no longer concerned Émile will interrupt the interrogation taking place. From the corner of my eye, I catch Émile refocusing his gaze on my profile.

"What happens when we figure out who's behind the threat and your services are no longer needed? Will I have to hunt you down for breaking Zaïre's heart?"

"I'll fix anything I break so your intervention won't be necessary. Besides, I plan on sticking around so there'll be no need to hunt for me."

"What happens to your company? Don't tell me you intend on selling."

I turn to Émile with one ear listening to Zaïre and Billy's current negotiation. "I can work just fine from anywhere. The way I see it, my future is here. And if need be, it ain't unheard of to move headquarters. There's more than enough incentive for me to relocate."

"I don't know how I feel about you going after my daughter. I didn't hire you for that."

"I met Zaïre before I knew she was any relation of yours. As much as I respect you and am indebted to you, I'm not willing to let anything separate us again. Not once I saw her sitting in your family room. And when we're in Bourbon, the rest of my family will understand why I won't be moving back when they meet her."

"If this is your way of asking for my blessing, you're doing a shitty job of it, you heard me."

I stare him down. "But you'll give it to me anyway because you know the kind of man I am, and ain't nobody out there that can compete with how good I'll be to her."

"Maybe y'all do deserve each other. Always trying to call me on shit. Can't you let me pretend to be a man at least once?"

If I didn't know him better, I would laugh at Émile's grumbling. No one can question his manhood; he ran a deadly motorcycle gang and still strikes fear in people with the wrong look.

I pound Hammer's shoulder. "Be comforted knowing I'm signing up for a lifetime of Zaïre calling me on my shit."

"Hmph. There's that at least."

"I'm done here," Zaïre says, surprising us. A curious

quality underlies her voice. She eyes us but doesn't vocalize the thoughts she hides.

Inwardly I cringe at the proof of my failure to watch over her because I was too busy trying to convince Émile my relationship with Zaïre isn't cause for concern. From the arch look he sends my way, he's made the same connection.

I turn towards the embalming table where Billy lies lifeless. "Did he say anything useful?"

"No names. Just a warning that I won't see my last day coming and other choice words I won't repeat."

"If you hadn't interfered—"

"What, Daddy? He would have told you? Taken you more seriously?"

"Perhaps not. Some people are loyal no matter how much torture they suffer. I never would have pegged Billy as one of them." Émile turns to the opening door.

We follow his stare to see Owl enter. She meets with Stealth and they begin a preparation of sorts on Billy's body. Just then it sinks in. The crematorium serves as a convenient cover to eliminate evidence tying the Flossers to murder.

Émile's eyes widen with the knowledge as well. "Well, I'll be…you've got yourself a sophisticated solution here," he says. With a nod and a pat on Zaïre's shoulder, he begins to walk away.

"Wait, Daddy. Don't you want to tell me everything you know now? Finding out who's after us will be a lot easier if we pool our resources. What do you know?"

"What I know is if you girls can find out whoever's at the center of this here conspiracy, y'all will have earned the Roudanez name. If y'all can do that, ain't nobody in the Bayou Hellraisers or anywhere else will give you any more shit, you heard me." He leaves a lot more calmly than he arrived.

I hold onto Zaïre's elbow to prevent her from following

him. From his tone, nothing she says will sway him into giving us more information. I don't know why it's so important to keep things secretive as it may endanger Zaïre and her sisters more than he thinks. But that's why I'm here. And unlike my earlier lapse, I will not allow Zaïre to walk into a trap without protection or a plan.

CHAPTER ELEVEN

Zaïre

*L*ucien and I head over to Cammy's main bike shop after a brief conversation with Owl and Stealth. The shop is an impromptu meeting place and where she goes to let off steam or to stop herself from murdering somebody. Whatever Darren and Smoke did to require me to step in with the Billy situation, they should count their blessings that they're still breathing.

Jojo and Thalie will meet us at the shop, and maybe I'll glimpse Darren's war wounds. But thoughts of my future meeting with my sisters keeps getting supplanted by the other conversation that took place at the crematorium. Although they kept their voices low, I heard what they said.

Even now, my mind replays the end of the conversation between my daddy and Lucien. As much as I try not to dwell on the effects on my body, the hot and cold sweat breaking out on my skin won't allow me to forget. My fear that he will leave me heartbroken seems to be all for nothing.

But now I don't know what to do with myself. Do I hug him and proclaim my feelings to the world? Or do I wait for the perfect moment? Will there even be a perfect moment? We have yet to identify the cause of my family's current predicament so how can I justify such a selfish act?

"Sweetheart, tell me what you're thinking." Lucien's eyes capture mine in the rearview mirror.

Instead of blurting out the truth my heart wants me to proclaim for the world to hear, I say, "Just contemplating who is close enough to my family that we won't see the threat coming before it's too late. Has Joel found any other leads?"

"Not yet. We probably lucked out when we discovered Billy because he was sloppy. I'm having Joel mine his life now to find an overlap. There has to be a connection we aren't seeing." Lucien's grip tightens around the steering wheel, turning his knuckles white.

We pull up to Cammy's shop and the tension in the air puts me on alert. "Oh, shit," I say.

Ann Wilson and Warren Haynes' guitar-heavy version of "You Don't Own Me" plays at full blast from the speakers, confirming my suspicions. "You Don't Own Me" is Cammy's go-to song to rage against the patriarchy or her inability to end someone's life. And if I know my sister, the song has been on repeat all damn day.

"What's wrong?" Lucien asks.

"I need a few minutes alone with my sister. Can you distract your brother?"

"Sure, but can I ask why?"

"I can't very well have my sister murdering her protection, now can I?"

"How do you know Darren is at fault?"

"I don't. It could be Smoke or both of them. Either way, give me the time I need to ensure *Darren's* safety."

Lucien's lips wobble as he suppresses a grin, but he nods his agreement.

We enter the garage where Darren stands guard. His stance is attentive, prepared for anything while wearing a relaxed smirk.

I shake my head at his naiveté.

Cammy mans a tubing bender for what looks to be the makings of a sick exhaust. Her face is set in a fierce, concentrated frown, but I know that is her outward appearance. Something is bothering her and if she doesn't get it off her chest soon, I am just as likely as a random person to suffer the brunt of her anger.

I brave an explosive temper by turning off the song to a chorus of yells. *Thank Gods* and *bless yous* echo from inside the shop and to the adjoined dealership.

Cammy's head swings in my direction, hell shooting sparks from her eyes until recognition hits and she schools her features. She steps away from her bender and I take her to her office and shut the door.

"What is happening?" I ask. "And don't try giving me a lame excuse. You and I know each other better than that."

Her shoulders slump. "Men suck ass."

"Is this about all men or one in particular?"

"How about all the above? If it ain't Daddy, it's Smoke. If not him, it's…"

"Who?" I ask although I already know.

Cammy paces the small confines of her office while I watch in growing confusion over her uncharacteristic behavior. "That man Daddy hired!"

"Let's hold off on what Daddy's done now to get on your shit list. What the hell did Smoke do?"

"You mean when he's not MIA? Whenever he finally

shows up, he acts like a Neanderthal and treats me like I'm incapable of stringing two thoughts together without his input. Things have just been off ever since you returned from Felicidad."

"Okay, he's another unresolved pain." I restrain from smiling at the signs that all is not well between her and Smoke. "What has Darren done to lump himself with Smoke and Daddy?"

Camille's complexion darkens and she avoids meeting my eyes.

"Cammy…"

"Do you know the shit that's on my plate? I run ten dealerships including this one, preside over the Flossers' business to make sure we keep getting more business, and I have to worry about who's coming for us. I don't have time for drama."

"Cammy…"

She throws up her arms. "The asshole kissed me like he owns me…and I…I didn't hate it. Fuck, I hate this shit. I didn't even push him away. God, he's so aggravating!" My sister pounds her fist into her hand. "I've never been unfaithful to Smoke and I wish I could forget what happened, but Darren is always around. And that godforsaken kiss stays on repeat in my head. I can't get any peace."

I hide the shock coursing through me. I'm going to hell because I kind of want Darren to do more. I don't know him well, but at this point, I'll snatch at any man who makes trouble for Cammy's relationship.

Not my proudest sister moment.

"Well, the sooner we figure out who is after us, the sooner he can go back where he came from," I lie.

I don't want him to leave if it means freeing Cammy from Smoke's influence. I give myself a pass this time because she won't hear anything past the guilt she feels about that kiss.

"You're right. The sooner he leaves, the sooner things between me and Smoke get back to normal." Cammy's enthusiastic agreement lacks conviction, but I play along by nodding my head.

"In the meantime, you're going to let him do his job, right?"

She turns on me with a glare. "I know you not trying to handle me right now like I'm a child."

"Definitely not."

"Because I can find a project to keep you busy."

"I'm good with the task you gave me." I grasp onto the subject because my sister will give me a shitty assignment that will have me cursing her name and rage fucking Lucien. "Actually, that's why I'm here," I say.

Cammy eyes me for endless seconds before she sits at her desk, the anger slowly fading away from her stiff muscles. "Yeah, what did you and Stealth find out from Billy?"

"Not a goddamn thing worth repeating. We still have no idea how he's connected to us or who put him up to kidnapping me, assuming I was his target."

"I'm sure you were. What now? Does your lover boy have a plan?"

I explain the conversation Lucien and I had on the ride over. "Another thing. Daddy showed up while I was questioning Billy so he knows we haven't been sitting on the sidelines. He gave us the green light to find out what's happening on our own."

"That's good, but we're so close to our next run next week and I can't help but feel uneasy with so many unknowns. We have something to prove with our first Oliveri shipment, and I've had several talks assuring him we won't fuck up. If only we hadn't agreed to ride with Smoke's crew, I'd rest easier."

"You think it's a Bayou Hellraiser behind everything?"

"I honestly don't know, but from what Joel discovered so

far, everyone in our circle came up clean. If it isn't someone in our house, everyone outside of it is sus."

"That would explain why Daddy's been so tight-lipped about information, but I still find it hard to believe. In all these years there hasn't been a whisper of dissatisfaction with our arrangement. Not to mention you're practically Smoke's Old Lady. If anyone has a vested interest in your safety, it's Smoke." All true. Although I don't want to believe Smoke would threaten us and would prefer to find another reason for Cammy to leave him, the suspicion has firmly lodged itself in the back of my mind.

"True. I'd hate to contemplate him being in on something this big. Still, let's get Joel a list of their members. If the Hell-raisers are behind the threat, I doubt they've involved their prospects."

"What about you? How's Darren handling your protection on the ride?"

A new flush suffuses Cammy's face. She turns to the paperwork on her desk, a frown of deep concentration furrowing her brow. "He's riding bitch," she says almost too casually.

"For the two days it'll take us to get to Bourbon? Shit, this trip is going to cause more problems if you join. Why don't you sit this one out?"

Cammy points a death stare at me.

"Roudanezes don't back down from nobody," we recite together.

"I don't even know why I suggested otherwise," I say. "I think it's time we invite the men in since we'll need their team to work on some of the logistics."

While Cammy and I discuss our theories, Jojo and Thalie arrive with their guards. With everyone present, we huddle in Cammy's office and share our suspicions about the Hell-raisers.

Lucien stands behind me, his hand resting on my waist. Gentle heat warms my belly with joy. He isn't even trying to hide his intentions.

I guess Daddy was the only obstacle to declaring himself, though how much of an obstacle Daddy presented remains to be seen. I subtly lean into Lucien's chest without outwardly appearing that I need him to prop me up. I do have an image to uphold, even if it's only for my sisters.

Ever since I overheard the last snippet of the conversation between Lucien and Daddy, I've been fighting to maintain my impression of the calm, collected VP the Flossers are accustomed to having. Difficult to do when I'm floating on air because Lucien eradicated any fear he will leave me heartbroken. My Big Tex ain't going nowhere. Damn, he wants to introduce me to the rest of the Connors family, and it's taking all my willpower not to smile until my face freezes.

"I already have Joel looking into Smoke," Darren says.

My sisters and I turn surprised gazes on Darren who is as imperturbable as ever. He has definitely caught my interest.

I can't do anything to get between Cammy and Smoke without risking our relationship, but Darren can.

"So far there's no connection with Billy, but I told Joel to keep digging until he finds it." Darren stares at Cammy as if daring her to undermine him.

"You suspected Smoke before today. Why are you so certain Smoke is behind this?" Cammy crosses her arms, aiming a scowl at Darren, who I am secretly rooting for with cheerleader pom-poms and all.

A look I can't identify crosses Darren's face. He leaves Cammy's question unanswered but doesn't leave off staring at her.

Carter clears his throat in the ensuing silence. "Speaking of Billy, I find it suspect that he only arrived in New Orleans a few months back. Did anything happen three to four months ago that you can remember?"

"It can be something you thought was odd at the time but since nothing came of it, you dismissed it," Lucien says.

Cammy relaxes her pose and I along with my sisters flip to the calendars on our phones as a way to trigger our memories. One after the other, we bring up minor incidents that occurred. We don't find a connection.

"Don't forget to consider Smoke's activities back then." Darren looms over Cammy after issuing his reminder.

My sister opens her mouth as if to blister him, but a thoughtful expression freezes her in place.

"What is it?" I ask.

"Maybe nothing. A few months ago, Smoke mentioned someone had contacted him through one of those family tree companies that link people through DNA. He never mentioned it again, so I figured he ignored it."

"Do you recall which company it was?" Blake asks.

"Find my...something...family? I think?"

My sister hasn't completed her thought before Darren types furiously on his phone. He raises his head to Lucien. "I'm reordering Joel's priorities. Got a problem with it?"

Is it fickle of me to be on team Darren? I don't expect him or Joel to find a connection with the threats against us, but I'm certain he can dig up enough dirt for my sister to move on. And honestly, if I hadn't realized that I'm in love with Lucien, Darren's quiet forcefulness might make me look twice.

Lucien considers his brother for a few tense seconds then nods his approval. We move on to discuss the planned stops along the run to Bourbon and our cover story for the Hellraisers who are still in the dark about the other reason for our run.

During the entire planning session, Lucien's body heat

seeps beneath my clothes, a reminder of his unquestioning support and belief in me. Whatever concerns I have no longer feel insurmountable, even with the unknown threat.

Fuck it, I don't care who sees my reaction or what it will do to my reputation. I link our hands at my waist and squeeze. He pulls me further into his body and I melt into him, ignoring the hard dick trying to drill a hole in my spine. I've got ideas for how to handle that later.

Thalie and Jojo arch their brows at me but say nothing in response when I confidently move closer to Lucien. Not that there is much closer for me to get.

I shrug but make no move to distance myself from the man who's stolen my heart despite my protests.

⚜⚜⚜

I follow closely behind Lucien as we enter my house, trying like hell to hide the devilish smile that wants to spread across my face. Ever since our meeting with my sisters, I've been toying with this idea to drive him crazy, to challenge some of that control he likes to hold over me, and to show him I'm all in with him.

I'll never be a completely submissive woman. The life I've built has made me too comfortable in being a leader, but nothing beats the inner glow I get whenever Lucien calls me "good girl".

I wait until after we've eaten dinner to make my move. He holds my hand as he leads me into the living room. The moment he pulls me to sit on his lap, I resist.

"I've been a good girl today and I want the reward I earned."

Lucien's brows rise in surprise before narrowing and filling with heat. This is the first time I've initiated this type of request.

"Really? How did you earn your good girl status today?"

I lick my lips and still the shudder that always travels through my body whenever he utters those words. Lowering my voice to a sensual whisper, I say, "I hid that very obvious erection you had during our entire meeting and didn't tease you once."

A smile bursts from his lips releasing those devastating dimples I've come to adore as much as the man himself. "I hate to break it to you sweetheart, but you being in the same room with me is a constant tease." He spread his knees wide and I follow his gaze to the prominent protrusion in his pants.

"You're only proving my point. If I'd acted on what I wanted to do to you, we would've had to reschedule our meeting."

His eyes sweep from my head down to my nipples poking through my red blazer to the juncture of my thighs currently hiding my clenching core. Everywhere his gaze touches adds more fuel to the banked fire of my desire.

"What reward do you think you've earned?" he rasps.

I slowly lick my lips, my eyes on the bulge that has grown larger while we talked, and I breathe, "Dessert."

His nostrils flare and his jaw clenches. "Fuck, siren. You really know how to tempt a man, but I have another reward in mind for you."

I step back, my hands on my hips. "What I want isn't up for debate."

Lucien closes the distance between us until he towers over me. "Are you forgetting how things work here, sweetheart?" He doesn't give me a chance to respond before I find myself over his shoulder and on my way to our bedroom.

"My job as your man is to take care of *all* your needs. Have you known me to neglect my pussy when she beckons me with her perfume?" He inhales deeply and tosses me on the bed.

"She can wait," I say, but not before Lucien strips me of my suit pants and underwear.

His intention is clear.

I roll away giggling while Lucien is in the middle of positioning himself. "This is ridiculous—"

"I agree. So get that sweet pussy on my mouth where she belongs, sweetheart." He stalks around the bed.

To buy myself more time with an escape from the room, I jump on the mattress. With one step to go, Lucien tackles me and we both tumble to the mattress. I am well and truly caught.

He rolls over and lifts me. Lucien never fails to surprise me with the ease which he manhandles my body. As if I weigh little more than a child. The closer he pulls my pussy to his mouth, the more I buck to get away. If his lips brush against me even once, I'll have lost this turn in our battle of wills.

At the last second, I cover his mouth with my hands. "Why can't we both have dessert at the same time?"

His grasp on my hips loosens, and I scoot backward. "I'm listening."

"I can't believe you're making me negotiate giving you a blowjob. If this is your pussy, that is my dick. And what does it say about *my* role in this relationship that I neglect *him* when he beckons to me?"

As I lay out my argument, the same one he gave me moments ago, I quickly undo his belt and pants, finally releasing the object of my obsession with an elated sigh. I'm so busy that I don't realize Lucien hasn't moved. I glance at him only to be caught in the raging inferno of his fierce stare.

"This is the second time you said something like that. I chalked up the first to you being in the heat of the moment, but I can't dismiss your words a second time." He grabs my neck, his stare intensifying. "Are you claiming my cock, siren? Because you need to know right now, there's no going back once you do."

"You saying I had a chance before?"

"Fuck, no. But I expected it to take longer before you realized."

"Consider this my claim." I gently squeeze his dick, smiling when he sucks in his breath. "Now, where were we?"

"You were about to feed me my dessert."

"That I was." I turn around and back my ass to his face.

His impatient hands grab my hips and pull me to his mouth where he latches onto my clit, pulling and sucking on the sensitive flesh. For uncountable seconds I am paralyzed, inundated with shock after shock of intense pleasure.

Cool air blowing on the hot bundle reminds me of my purpose. I lower my face and inhale Lucien's addictive scent. He is the only man I know who uses wet wipes between full showers. "To ensure I'm always fresh for you," he said the first time I remarked on it. Lucien's tongue delves into my pussy, the sign I need to catch up, or else he'll have me coming way sooner than he does.

I begin to lick and stroke, but any game plan I have to make him lose control falls by the wayside with the first taste of his pre-cum on my tongue. The scent of his skin causes me to lose myself, while the feel of his hot, steely length and savory flavor drown me in ecstasy. I suck and swallow eagerly.

I used to think I had to be stage director, fully in control of my pleasure in the bedroom until Lucien showed me I was playing a small off-Broadway production. He runs a full show and he knows how to make me perform to my fullest. He can be so domineering. But at times like this, when I hold him in my hands or suck on him, he becomes my equal partner in pleasure.

I am close, my body clenches uncontrollably. He is too. His moans become more guttural, his balls begin to draw up. I succumb to the impulse that has been chasing me since our helicopter date, and say, "I love you," uncaring that his dick muffles the words. I am compelled to free the words from their captivity.

Although Lucien might not understand the muffled gibberish, he comes hard, coating my throat with his hot cum. Not one to be left behind, Lucien's mouth closes over my clit and the suction is so powerful I join him in an over-whelming orgasm. I topple to the side so as not to suffocate him but he rolls with me, hugging my hips to his face and applying soft kisses to my pussy while my body calms.

When new desire sparks to life between my thighs, I push away from him. My freedom only lasts long enough for Lucien to pull me face-to-face with him. He pushes my twists away from my forehead and kisses me. There is nothing this man does to me I don't love.

"For the record," I say with my hand on his hardening dick, "This is my preferred reward."

"Duly noted." Instead of following through on what his reawakening body wants, Lucien grasps my hand and lays it over his heart, and kisses my eyelid. "Make sure to pack a nice outfit for the run to Bourbon. As much as I love you in leather, I don't think it's the best for a first impression with my parents."

"Are they flying in specifically to meet me?"

A small smile spreads across his face, his dimple setting the butterflies in my chest aflutter. "No, sweetheart. My family's lived in Bourbon almost as long as there's been a Bourbon, Texas."

"How am I just now finding this out?"

He shrugs. "We'll have a lifetime to discover everything there is to know about each other. What's the rush?"

I clear the lump in my throat. I've only just come to terms with my feelings, not the long-term relationship Lucien is talking about. "What do I need to do to get their approval?"

Lucien turns us on our sides and grasps my nape to glare ferociously into my eyes. "You've got it wrong, sweetheart. You meeting them isn't me seeking their approval. It's a courtesy. They need to meet the reason I'm not returning to Texas. You see, the men in my family have a well-known affliction that's been passed down from generation to generation. When we meet our one and only, we know it immediately. And there ain't nothing anyone can do or say to sway us. Hell, my dad will wonder what's taken me so long to lock you down."

I scoff, finding it hard to believe this man who is so grounded in reality could fall for such a romantic fantasy.

"It's true sweetheart. My mom and dad's second date was their wedding. So far he holds the record for shortest courtship. You and me will likely be one of the longest hold-outs." A frown mars his beautiful mouth but disappears almost instantly, leaving me questioning who else was holding out. "As all my uncles and grandfather married their wives within a week to a month of knowing each other, you'll understand if I get impatient."

"You've gotten me to agree to a lot of things, but I can't remember agreeing to marry you."

"Which is the only reason it's taking so long. While we're on the subject, I'm putting you on notice. The second after you agree to be my wife, your ass will be in front of a judge saying I do. We can have the fancy wedding later because I ain't breathing another breath as a single man a moment longer than I have to." He pushes me on my back. "Until then,

I'll do my damnedest to convince you it's a good idea to give me what I want."

He spreads my legs and thrusts inside me, stealing my breath. For the rest of the night, he follows through on his word, working my body over in a slow dance of passion. All the air in my body is reserved for pleading. Pleading for more, for him to fuck me harder. Slower. Deeper. All while the word I want to say is yes. Yes to forever with him. Yes to being his wife. But what is taking too long for him is still too soon for me.

CHAPTER TWELVE

Lucien

*O*ther than a few skirmishes within the Hellraisers' crew that get handled with brutal efficiency, the ride to Bourbon is uneventful. Yet unease skates along my spine, clinging to me like an infatuated flea. No matter how many preparations my team put in place there is always the possibility we missed something. That *I* missed something. And I can't afford to fuck up.

I glance at Zaïre riding beside me with her cat in his pink leather jacket and riding goggles sitting cooler than sweet tea on a summer's day behind her. Tux turns to me, and I imagine he's preening beneath the lenses. Even though he's warmed to me, Tux doesn't let an opportunity slide if he can remind me he'll always be a priority for Zaïre.

As for my siren, we've gotten used to riding together, our signals display our seamless communication. Her confidence on the bike sparks pride in my chest. She is mine. My present and my future and although she hasn't agreed yet, I've let her know in no uncertain terms she has no alternative. Soon she'll open up all the way and confess the feelings that shine through her hazel eyes.

More now than ever, I need to be on my game. I called every off-duty CESP operator to ensure Zaïre and her sisters survive this run. My people staff the agreed-upon checkpoints across the route and secure our lodgings the Flossers reserved along the way. Everything under my control is working as intended.

Except my brother who has never been mine to command.

I swear, the asshole means to rile Smoke up for a fight. And whatever excuse Camille gave her boyfriend to explain their separate sleeping quarters hasn't helped matters.

With Joel working on connecting Smoke with the man Zaïre interrogated, I don't agree with Darren's actions. But my brother is an equal partner. I can't fire or replace him. If I try, Darren would tell me to fuck off and continue to protect the woman he's been fixated on since he arrived in New Orleans.

It's what I'd do.

Despite Zaïre's belief that Smoke would never threaten Camille or those she loves, my gut tells me Smoke is our man. I just need the proof, but Smoke isn't cooperating.

Two towns outside of Bourbon, we separate from the Bayou Hellraisers. We break into smaller crews, taking alternate routes to the night's motel to confuse anyone who may look for us along the way. Each crew also rides a circuitous route with no rhyme or reason. Our methods are meant to lose anyone currently trailing us. As an added precaution, I've stationed lookouts who will call me in case we have a tail.

It takes us another ninety minutes to arrive at our destination, but the extra time is worth it because no one has followed us. As we pull in, I notice the building for the first time. There's nothing classy about this place, but we don't need class for the kind of business Zaïre intends to conduct on this run. At least it's clean.

Once all the women separate into their rooms, I complete my safety rounds and check in with my men. All the Roudanez sisters are safe, though my brother may not last the night if the threats I hear from Camille's door are any indication. I shake my head as I walk to the suite I share with Zaïre.

The delivery drop doesn't happen for another two days, so tomorrow she'll meet my parents. One less day on the countdown of her single status.

My phone rings, halting my steps. "Are your eyes still on the target?"

"I'm sorry, Lucien. I thought he was in for the night, but I got an itch at the back of my neck so I decided to check on him. His bike is here but he isn't in his room."

"Have any taxis picked up any passengers?"

"Shit. A taxi showed up about twenty minutes ago. I'll try to track it down and call you back with any info I get."

I hang up on my man and double back to Darren and Camille's room. Darren opens the door wide for my entry. I search for Camille who upon glancing at my face straightens from what I imagine is an attack pose.

"What happened? Is it Zaïre?"

"Your sister is fine for the moment. I've lost eyes on Smoke. Does he have a way to track you?" Both Darren and I train our attention on Camille.

"No. Darren switched out my phone for a burner before we left New Orleans. I've never even called Smoke on it. I still think you're barking up the wrong tree here. Smoke doesn't have a reason to hurt me."

"Do you think he planted a tracker on the bikes?" Darren asks me. From the fire in his eyes, he doesn't like how quick Camille is to defend our prime suspect.

"Stay here," I tell Camille. "Darren and I will check everyone's bike just in case."

"Fine. My sisters will be here when you're done."

Darren and I take flashlights and inspect the motorcycles but come up with nothing. Not discovering any GPS trackers should ease my concerns, but Smoke's continued disappearance remains a specter over my head.

Next, we check on the delivery. They call their Road Captain, Chaperone. She and Stealth guard the Flossers' shipment. I never asked what Zaïre is delivering, on whose behalf, or to whom she will offload the goods. It ain't none of my business. But I'm confirming it's getting the proper attention now to ensure no one fucks up Zaïre and Camille's plans.

The click of two, maybe four guns precedes Chaperone and Stealth's appearance from the shadows.

"I know you two are working for our First Lady and VP but that don't give you the right to nose in on business that ain't yours." Stealth points her guns behind me and Darren. "Now why don't you do what you were hired for and let us do what we do best?"

"I'm glad you take your jobs seriously," I say, somewhat relieved that they aren't slacking off this close to their delivery date. "We're here to give you a heads up. Smoke's missing. It'll be a good idea to assign more people on watch until we find him or whatever the hell he's up to."

"Appreciate the warning. Now, why don't you step away before I get nervous?" Stealth's steady gaze and confident hold betray the lie.

A healthy dose of respect has me nodding at her, glad

she's one of Zaïre's people. If she ever got nervous, I doubt there will be survivors.

We leave but not before I hear Stealth's voice addressing another member to get their asses on duty. Darren and I return to Camille's room where I collect Zaïre. I need her close to me. Because although we found nothing and Stealth looks to have things in hand, my gut tells me the situation will only get more dangerous.

CHAPTER THIRTEEN

Zaïre

*L*ast night Lucien's tension caused me to doze instead of falling into a deep sleep. Every hour to two hours he checked on everything, from inspecting areas for potential ambush to calling in status updates with all his men. If he hadn't shown me his dedication to my safety before, last night cinched it for me. But I hate the purple discoloration under his emerald eyes, evidence of his sleepless night.

From his and Darren's reaction to Smoke going off the grid, I have to believe there's something there. They aren't biased like I am, at least Lucien isn't. And he didn't get to where he is by ignoring his gut. But if I'm honest with myself, the situation with Smoke isn't my foremost concern. That would be my upcoming dinner with Lucien's parents.

The objections that should have crossed my mind before are now taking turns to slam my face into how improbable being with Lucien is. He comes from old money. And not the kind that foists their kids onto nannies and boarding schools. His family was there for him every time he needed them. They give him emotional and financial support without question. Hell, they even socialize with senators and presidents without having to use coercive measures unlike me.

Why would they accept me and my very illegal way of life when Lucien can do better?

"Sweetheart, I don't know what you're thinking but I have a feeling I won't like it." Lucien interrupts my doubt spiral, a scowl marring his forehead. "Get your ass over here and give me a taste of my favorite thing."

"I am not riding your face before I meet your mother."

A grin trembles on his lips. "My other favorite thing then." He pulls my body into his and steals my soul through a tender kiss. It lasts even after I've melted into his body and feathered my fingers through the hairs at his neck. It lasts until we're at the point of passing out from lack of oxygen.

When we separate, gasping into each other's mouths, I can't look away from his lips. I wait just long enough to refill my lungs before leaning in for another kiss.

"I much prefer this look on your face." Lucien pulls away and grins.

My eyes are probably glassy with passion and I'm certain I look half drunk. I roll my eyes because with one kiss Lucien dashes my doubts into the air. It doesn't matter if my family is more like the Black Coreleones than the Kennedys. I lean forward for another taste of Lucien, one of *my* favorite things, when a knock sounds at the door.

We groan in unison.

"Lucien, I need to talk to you before you leave," Darren's voice filters through the door.

Lucien sets me aside and rises. He stalls me when I move

to follow. "Finish getting dressed, and I'll fill you in when I get back."

"You're lucky I trust you," I shoot back on my way to the bathroom with Tux on my heels.

"Trust is the foundation for a strong marriage," he responds.

I flip him the bird behind my back and laugh at his obvious ploy. I turn my attention to getting ready. Lucien only has to style his hair while I still have to shower, dress, and do my makeup.

While I apply my lipstick, Lucien enters. He rests against the door and whistles his appreciation. "You look amazing."

"Well, you look sleep-deprived. Too handsome for your own good, but sleep-deprived nonetheless."

I go into the bathroom and reenter the bedroom with a wet washcloth. With his hand in mine, I lead him to the bed, push him down, and crawl behind him. "Hush and let me take care of you for once. We have time before we need to leave." I spread my legs and pull at his shoulder until he lays his head on my lap.

Lucien closes his eyes and sinks into me. "You trying to show me what heaven feels like?"

"Don't I do that every day? Heaven is wherever I am, did you forget?"

"Nah, but hearing you acknowledge it does my heart good."

"Boy, let me tend to you and not your foolishness." I place the cool, damp cloth across his eyes. "I'm not gonna have your mama looking at me sideways because she doesn't know why you aren't sleeping properly."

"My mom married a Connors man. She'll know why I'm not sleeping." Lucien rubs my thigh in sensual circles.

"Why don't you tell me what your brother wanted instead

of trying to seduce my panties off me?" I massage his brow, happy when he sighs and sinks deeper into my caress.

"If I must," he moans, pulls my leg over his shoulder, and nuzzles my inner thigh. "Darren wanted to remind me he isn't coming to dinner with us and to bitch at me about Joel's progress, or lack thereof. I can't blame Darren, though. The sooner we confirm or dismiss Smoke as a suspect the sooner we can concentrate our efforts elsewhere."

"I don't understand why he would want to eliminate us. Daddy still has a lot of pull with the Hellraisers. I can't imagine the other members being on board."

"It could be anything, but I'm inclined to think maybe Smoke isn't doing too well as Émile's successor. He's probably got a lot to prove in a well-established organization. To see you and your sisters start yours from scratch *and* succeed at it must burn his chaps."

"Don't get me wrong, I've always had reservations about Smoke, but shouldn't he celebrate Cammy's accomplishments? You would never want me to fail even if we were competitors," I say with all confidence.

"That's because real men know when to take a back seat. Your success can never threaten me since the most important thing I live for is to share your happiness. And that ain't no one-time thing. I want a lifetime of your joy."

This man.

Lucien is a smooth talker, but he's honest. And his sincerity turns me into a marshmallow. I reward him by lowering my mouth to his for an awkward upside-down kiss.

"We should probably leave soon, or we'll be late." I remove the now warm cloth from his face.

With one last squeeze of my leg, he rises and puts the finishing touches on his appearance. We take a cab to his parents' home. Now, New Orleans has many stately homes with a lot of history behind their fluted columned entrances, but the Connors' residence puts them to shame in acreage and architectural style. Remnants of my earlier doubts begin to whisper in my ear until Lucien kisses my knuckles.

"Come on, sweetheart. It's time to meet your future in-laws."

"Lucien…" Why am I even pretending that his vision of us won't happen? Lucien gets what he wants, and this time our wants are the same.

He opens the cab's door and pulls me after him. At the entrance to the house, he raises his hand to knock but the door swings open and an older woman with Lucien's coloring pulls him inside for a maternal hug and scolding.

"You're finally home! Why must my boys go gallivanting off to the ends of the earth with barely a warm word for their mother?"

"I'm literally one state over, Ma."

"One state might as well be another planet. Oh, how I missed my baby."

I grin at the thought of anyone calling Lucien a baby with his overgrown self.

"If you let me go for five seconds, I'd like to introduce you to someone." He gently pulls away from his mother's embrace.

Lucien's mother gasps and peers around him until she spies me. A broad grin exposes her white even teeth and the dimple she passed down to her son. "You brought me a daughter?"

My eyes round in shock at her assumption and immediate acceptance.

"I can't rightly say that yet. Although she hasn't said no, she hasn't said yes either." Lucien's drawl thickens while he talks to his mother. "Ma, this is Zaïre. Zaïre, this here is Lorraine Connors, the best mother a man can ask for. And she makes a mean pecan pie." Lucien delivers a sloppy kiss to his mother's cheek.

"My boy just likes to brag. Come on in. Let me show you around and introduce you to my husband, Ethan. By the way"—she pokes Lucien in the chest—"where is that other no-good son of mine? I thought he would be with you."

"He's working on a personal project. He has high hopes he'll get her to see things his way soon."

I turn startled eyes to Lucien who shrugs. Was he referring to my sister as Darren's personal project? I didn't expect his feelings to be that serious so soon, but if he's anything like his brother, his actions make sense.

Lorraine grips my hand and tows me inside the vast space in which she raised Lucien and Darren. History lives in these walls, but I can't say I'm brave enough to ask for a lesson, preferring to judge the Connors on their actions and not those of their ancestors.

Lucien's father, Ethan, emerges from what appears to be a den to greet us. He is an older version of Lucien with blond hair a few shades lighter than his son and just as welcoming as his wife.

He engulfs me in a warm hug. "Have you hired a planner yet?" Ethan directs the question to Lucien who smirks unabashedly. "Oh, it's like that, is it?"

"I'm hoping you and Ma'll help me convince her." Lucien winks at me as if he hasn't just waved a red flag at two overly enthusiastic charging bulls.

Thankfully, my belly makes its emptiness known with a rumble and Lorraine ushers us to an outdoor eating area set for four. Throughout the meal Ethan and Lorraine more often than not are touching each other, their love still palpable after many years together. The hours speed away from us until it's time to leave.

"Well, sweetheart? Am I any closer to getting a yes from

you?" Lucien nuzzles the side of my neck in the taxi's back-seat on our return to the motel.

"Ha! You think you're slick. If I say yes now, you'll take it as a final yes and have me in front of a judge before I can say my full legal name."

He pulls away to stare intently into my eyes. "Would that be so bad?"

I caress his cheek. "Don't rush things. What will happen will happen when it's supposed to, no sooner."

He kisses my palm. "Until then, I'll do my utmost to steer the future where I want it. Because sometimes fate needs a nudge."

Lucien's plans to prod us in the direction he wants to take our relationship are put on hold the minute we see Darren pacing at our door.

CHAPTER FOURTEEN

Lucien

*A*s soon as Darren enters the motel room I share with Zaïre, he burst out, "Joel found the link between Smoke and Billy."

Ever since my brother "rearranged" Joel's priorities, he's been making a nuisance of himself, pestering our man for updates twice a day. Darren, too keyed up to sit still, paces the small room. His pacing disturbs Tux and the cat jumps on the desk in front of the window overlooking the parking lot to observe us.

Zaïre and I sit on the bed. "Why isn't Cammy with you? My sister should be part of this conversation."

Darren's nostrils flare. "I shared the news with her already. She said she needed to talk to Stealth."

A knock at the door prevents me from taking him to task for leaving Zaïre's sister unprotected. "It's me," Camille enters, but there's something off about the way she carries herself. As if, for the first time, she realizes she's misplaced her faith in Smoke, and she's struggling to smother her feelings for him under her obligations to her family and crew. "Jojo and Thalie are taking shifts protecting the goods."

Zaïre pulls her sister onto the bed next to her and holds her hand. No judgment, just support.

"Are you going to keep us in suspense or tell us what he found?" I ask Darren. It's not a ploy to get the information, but to give Camille time to absorb the reality of our situation.

"Billy found Smoke through a company called Find My Ancestry. He was someone's secret baby and he had a real shitty home life growing up so when he found out he had more family, he sought them out. Apparently, *Smoke*," Darren sneers, "Didn't ignore the call Camille told us about. I had Joel check because I don't believe in that big of a coincidence."

"Okay, so we have his connection to Billy. We still don't know why he's after my family." Anger and frustration underlie Zaïre's words.

"We may not find that out until we find Smoke." I rub her shoulders to soothe the tension building there.

"Did he return to the motel between yesterday and today?" Darren asks.

"Not as of the time we left for dinner. But I'm due another update." As soon as the words leave my mouth my phone rings. I put it on speakerphone so I won't have to repeat the conversation.

"Where is he?" I spit out.

"He's still not back yet and I think it's because something big is about to go down. A few of the prospects and newer members left the motel this morning and haven't returned. Now, they may be off doing official Hellraiser business, but this situation doesn't seem kosher."

"You're right, it isn't. Wait for my call before you do anything. I want to confirm something first." I hang up without waiting for a response and turn to Zaïre and Camille. "Call your father. He might know if what's going on is business as usual."

If there's one thing I've learned since my days as a Delta Force operator, it's information and preparation are the key to bringing everyone on my team home alive. There are too many unknowns and we're in an impossible situation. My only course of action now is to get as much intel as possible and regroup with another plan.

Like me, Zaïre puts her call on speaker. "Daddy, do you know where Smoke is?"

"Now I know I raised you better than this. I don't get no proper greeting?" Émile's grumpy voice sounds over the speaker.

"Hi, Daddy. Should I call Mama to get you to answer me?"

"One of these days, invoking your mama's name isn't gonna work, you heard me."

"Is today that day, Daddy?"

"Humph. I haven't seen Smoke going on two days now. But why are you asking about him instead of your sister? Where is she?"

"Don't worry about where I am," Camille says. "I'm aware of what's happening. There's something else we need to know. The members and prospects that went out this morning but haven't returned yet, were they on official club business?"

"Now, why you want to ask about our members? You know our business ain't for the public. From what I can tell, your club operates the same way."

"Hammer, we don't care what the Bayou Hellraisers' official business is as long as it doesn't put your daughters at risk," I say. "And before you put us off, we found out Billy and

Smoke are family. Now we need to know if he's using anyone else in the club to target your daughters."

"Nah, whoever told you that is playing on your top. Smoke would never. Not after I helped him become president."

"And how is he doing at the job?" Darren asks.

"That there's Hellraiser business, you heard me."

"Daddy, decide now whether you want to be more loyal to your club or your family." Camille's hardened voice tells everyone she won't bend if her father doesn't take her seriously as he's done in the past.

"I know the club is your baby, but last I checked, we didn't do nothing to warrant being on the Hellraiser's shit list," Zaïre says.

"Why you gotta talk to your daddy like that? You know I'd never put the club above your safety. But Smoke…he's going to be my son-in-law."

I don't miss the catch in Émile's voice. Neither does Camille from the way she looks everywhere but at the phone or Darren.

"Like hell he is!" Darren bursts out, his fists clenching. "You need to be a better judge of character. And there's no way that piece of shit is ever going to marry your daughter."

"Now's not the time to debate that," I say, shaking my head when Darren opens his mouth as if to protest. "Give us something that helps us keep your family safe," I tell Émile.

"When you put it like that…Everyone on official business came back hours ago. We were supposed to have Church today to hear some big announcement, but with Smoke missing, it's been put off."

"Do you have any idea what the announcement was going to be?" I tense, not liking where Émile is going.

"Something about a new supplier. I think we're expecting a delivery, but it's been kept pretty hush-hush."

Zaïre and Camille's widened eyes meet mine and Darren's.

"You've got no idea what's in the shipment or where the drop is supposed to be?" Zaïre asks. She mouths to me that her father doesn't know about this delivery.

"No. I'm lucky to know what I do since I'm no longer running things, and I've used up all my resources. I've got nothing else to tell you."

Again, I don't believe all these events aren't connected. Somehow Smoke found out about the Flossers' delivery, but due to their precautions, our destination never leaked.

"Thanks, Hammer. It's more useful than you think." I nod to Zaïre to hang up.

She immediately dials another number. Stealth's voice filters through the speakers like she's in a tunnel.

"Stealth, have Mama Bear take over guarding the shipment then bring me Smoke. I don't care what you have to do to get him here. Make sure he's alive but immobile."

"Uh…Mama Bear is in place and I'm already on my way…"

We all look at Camille, and I recall Darren's comment about her leaving to have a conversation with Stealth.

"He may not be alone, so be careful," Camille says, ignoring all our stares. As if sending Stealth after someone isn't significant. And for that someone to be Smoke…

I remember how quickly Stealth produced results with Billy. The memory provides some reassurance, but until we have eyes on him and the missing members, I won't rest easy. I watch Zaïre hug her sister. I'll do whatever it takes to ensure my worst-case scenario doesn't come true because losing Zaïre will end me.

CHAPTER FIFTEEN

Zaïre

*W*e spend all night in the room I share with Lucien going over plans to counter the unknown; an impossible task. I should be freaking out, but Lucien's presence beside me acts as a balm to my anxiety.

We take a break from round after round of what-ifs, knowing we'll pick up again in a few minutes. Darren and Cammy leave to get us snacks and beverages, which reminds me that dinner was many hours ago. Lucien and I change into more comfortable clothes, and he draws me into his embrace on the bed against the headboard.

Tux, who was sleeping on the desk while we planned, stretches and jumps into my lap and rubs his head against my chin.

"As much as I'd like to assume the quiet means Smoke doesn't know where we are, I can't trust he won't know the location for the handoff." I achieve a calm, measured tone because Lucien is with me, planning alongside me; an equal partner.

"It's too late to change now, but we have to assume the route we planned on using is compromised as well. This town will limit our options since we need to hide in plain sight and there's only one section where your bikers won't raise eyebrows."

"I think this place was chosen because it's a small town. It's easy to stand out, but it's also easy to hide some dark shit." An idea sparks in my head. "Wait a minute. Since you grew up here, you've got to know some way around the major thoroughfares."

Lucien rubs his stubbled chin on my cheek, humming in deep thought. "If our biggest challenge is hiding your presence, the best way to do that is not to ride your bikes to the drop-off. We'll also have to change that trailer…"

I sit in comfortable silence as Lucien continues to work things out in his head. Cammy and Darren return with a treasure trove of junk food and sodas. As they unload their find, I notice Cammy stands a lot closer to Darren than she's ever willingly done before. There's also redness in her eyes as if she's been crying.

My gaze shoots up to Darren who shakes his head, warning me not to bring attention to the signs of my sister's distress. Lucien squeezes my waist and I settle down. I can wait until I get Cammy alone to find out what happened.

"We're too late to change the drop-off, but I've got an idea that can get us there safely," Lucien says.

"Does it involve the Connollys?" Darren asks.

Both Cammy and I question, "Who are the Connollys?"

"Darren and I grew up with them. Their family founded Bourbon., and the town reveres them as the unofficial first family. But the kids we grew up with play by different rules, and they have no problems dirtying their hands if it adds a little danger to their otherwise safe lives."

Lucien shares his plan with us. From Darren's nods, he thinks the plan will work, too. The brothers reach out to the Connolly family. Cammy and I watch as the brothers joke around with the men who just might save us from an ambush on the road.

Cammy finds herself beside me and we clasp hands, our grip tightens the longer we wait to hear if we have to come up with a less workable plan. Darren and Lucien finally get around to the purpose of their conversation. From their nodding heads, hope blossoms in my chest.

"Well, sweetheart, you've got yourself some new partners." Lucien rubs my shoulder reassuringly. With a new alternative on the table, Cammy calls an impromptu meeting with the members assigned to make the run and we tell them the change in plans.

When everyone files out leaving the four of us, Darren says, "We should use the next couple hours to get some rest. Camille and I will regroup with you and Zaïre before the Connollys arrive."

Lucien walks them to the door and closes it behind them. "He's right. You need to sleep or your reaction time will suffer."

I set my alarm and hold my hand out to him. "Your reaction time will suffer, too."

He takes my hand and we crawl into bed. Sleep soon overtakes us, but it isn't restful.

❧❧❧❧

My crew waits anxiously behind the motel for the Connolly brothers and their men. Ten of them show up armed and ready to aid us. I don't know what these

Connollys are into, but I know when to ask questions, and now is definitely not the time. We quickly transfer Oliveri's goods from our trailers into the four empty horse trailers the Connollys brought. The crates fit surprisingly well within the partitions, which ensures they won't move around in transit.

I catch Darren and Cammy whispering off to the side. Her worried frown compels me to ask her what's up.

"I told Stealth to check in with me every few hours. She's missed two calls with me now."

"Should I send someone to look for her?" I am as concerned as Cammy about Stealth's silence. She is our most effective enforcer and works great solo, but she knows better than to cut off communication with Cammy.

Although she keeps her personal life separate from Flosser business, Cammy and I've met her husband. An Boa Luong's empire is immense, and so are his connections to the underworld. He isn't one to fuck with, and no one means more to him than Stealth. If we don't find her first, our club risks being crushed into oblivion.

Cammy hums as if going through the list of members. "I'll send Mama Bear—"

"We need her for the decoy trip. We might trick Smoke that we're the ones on our bikes, but we don't have anyone else Mama Bear's size, and he won't buy a fake."

"Shit… I'll go." Cammy nods her head, her lips thinned in determination. "You stay with the delivery since you're the face they'll recognize. If you don't show, there's no way we'll get repeat business with Gio."

"Do I get a say in this shitty plan?" Darren asks.

"No," Cammy and I say at the same time.

"Stealth is family. And her silence means she's in trouble." Cammy approaches a member who is supposed to stay and guard our belongings at the motel.

Darren follows closely on her heels.

My mind wanders to Stealth. If Cammy is worried enough to show it, the situation is serious. With one last prayer for my sister to find Stealth and get to safety, I head to my designated horse trailer.

Our decoy convoy with the empty trailers leaves half an hour before we do. They'll follow the route from our initial plans. At the last minute, they'll divert to a new location hoping to lead Smoke's people away from our drop-off.

Now that the time to move is upon me, sweat runs down my back, but I can't delay this any longer. I signal for everyone to move. Lucien, to reassure himself, checks my body armor, and I check his. Although Kevlar can't protect us from all bullets, wearing it provides an added layer of security.

Blake and Jojo, Thalie and Carter, and Lucien and I pair up to man three trailers. The Connolly brothers drive the last one in our procession. Their men stand guard inside with the cargo, two for each trailer. I don't like trusting these strangers with such a sensitive delivery, but I have no other choice thanks to Smoke.

Lucien sits behind the wheel with one hand resting reassuringly on my thigh and his eyes sweeping the streets. "When we've honored your commitment with this delivery, we'll go after Smoke ourselves. I hate playing defense and it's time we become the hunter."

"We'll have to be careful. Daddy's still a Hellraiser. We can't start a war we can't finish."

"If that's your only concern, then you don't have to be part of it. I have no problem ending him on my own. With my resources, no one will connect anyone in the Roudanez family to his permanent disappearance."

"Aren't you a sweet talker all of a sudden? As much as I appreciate the sentiment, and I do, unless we know what's driving him, we can't ever be certain someone else won't target us for the same reasons."

My phone rings and I put it on speaker. "Hey Veep," Mama Bear shouts over the noise on the road. "We had a few tails on our ass but when we veered away from the drop location, they didn't follow us."

"How many were there?" Lucien asks.

"Half a dozen, maybe?"

"There were twice as many missing from their motel. Thanks for the update Mama Bear. We're going to need you to back us up. Ditch the trailers as soon as possible and meet us at the drop. I'm almost certain there'll be trouble." I hang up and turn to Lucien. "Any more bright ideas?"

"None come to mind. But whatever goes down, you're walking out of there alive, sweetheart. I won't accept any other outcome." He squeezes my thigh.

The closer we get to our destination the more my muscles tense. There's no sign anyone is following us. The horse trailers seem to be an effective cover from ambush, but there's still more time in the day for Smoke to fuck us over.

We turn onto a dirt road in the middle of nowhere. The last building we passed was five miles away and its dilapidated state speaks to having been abandoned years ago. Rocky outcroppings and tall cacti pepper the landscape, enough to provide cover to anyone with the right weapon. We pull up to our destination, an industrial-sized barn, and wait.

A tense two minutes pass. A familiar figure from my conversation with Gio appears at the entrance. Tate, Gio's customer, wears a cowboy hat and chews on a toothpick. I nod to Lucien and exit the trailer, but signal for everyone else to stay until we're ready for the exchange.

"Your photo doesn't do you justice." Tate leers at me, but I ignore the look. "Did you encounter any problems getting here?"

"No, but we'll have to make this quick. A rival club's been trying to get intel on us and I can't guarantee they don't know about this place."

"Then let's do this."

I gesture for my sisters, their guards, and the Connollys to open the trailers. Tate inspects the first crate of goods. We face away from them, not needing to know what's in the delivery.

"Looks like we have a deal." Tate calls to another of his men who appears with two large aluminum briefcases.

I open the case and inspect the stacks of cash. Counting it here isn't feasible, but I make damn sure the denominations are the same in both cases before snapping them closed. "It was wonderful doing business with you. Be on the lookout for a dozen men who're looking for trouble." I describe Smoke to them, leaving out the Hellraiser name. If Smoke starts shit, I don't want it blowing back on my daddy.

"Thanks for the heads up. We'll leave first." Tate and his men make quick work of the transfer and leave a trail of dust on their way off the property.

"Well that was anticlimactic," Thalie says sidling next to me. "I bet Cammy wishes she could have been here."

"We aren't safe until we're back in our territory." I check my phone for missed calls from our sister, but there aren't any. My unease, which has been on a low simmer, boils to the surface. I call Cammy, but there's no answer.

"We got company." Lucien's warning is barely in time before shots ricochet off the trailer.

Some bullets thud into the metal. From the high-velocity impact, our opponents have high-caliber assault weapons, which will render our Kevlar useless.

We scatter behind the semis, using them as shields against

the onslaught of bullets. I glance over to make sure Thalie is safe. Carter has her pressed against the trailer, one hand pressed against the trail of blood running down his arm. My sister has two guns out and ready for anyone unlucky enough to get in her sights.

She reminds me I'm not completely helpless and have weapons to defend myself, too. I can only assume Jojo is doing the same. From the lack of responding fire, everyone is in the same position as Lucien and me. We don't have a visual and we aren't willing to waste our ammo by shooting blindly.

"Where are your men?" I ask Lucien.

"The bastards must have killed them." Grief brackets his mouth.

I reach out to him, knowing the gesture offers scant consolation. Lucien takes the welfare of his men personally and if they are dead as he suspects I can't imagine how he will recover.

Smoke and his men stop shooting, probably realizing they aren't achieving the desired result of murdering us.

"Zaïre," he yells. "If you want to walk out of here alive, all you gotta do is hand over the money."

Rage like nothing I've experienced before washes over me, but one head shake from Lucien tempers my knee-jerk response. Of course, I can't act recklessly, not after Lucien lost men. "Tell me why. You're supposed to be in love with my sister!"

"She was a tool to get me the presidency." Smoke's voice comes from our left. With all the brush and rock structures surrounding us, we can't get a good visual of him.

"Keep him talking," Lucien whispers to me.

I nod. "She has to be more than that. You've been president for over a year." If not for the threat of being shot, I might have run out to confront the asshole who wasted my sister's time on a lie.

From the corner of my eye, I see Lucien motion to the Connollys' men. They nod and disappear around their trailers one by one.

"Yeah, and she kept showing me up. My woman must know her place. I can't have a female more successful than me. Your Flossers shouldn't even exist, and I was always going to end the cooperation deal you worked out with Hammer." Smoke's voice now comes from our right.

"Then why'd you wait to act?"

Lucien and I share a look. How is Smoke able to move without us spotting him? There isn't even a hint of rustling in the dry vegetation surrounding us.

"Your father still holds a lot of sway with the old guard, and our treasurer has been asking questions about our funds. I have big ideas for the club that require capital. Then Camille let it slip she was talking to Gio Oliveri. That was the last straw. The Bayou Hellraisers deserve that deal, not some fledgling female club. I couldn't let that shit stand."

Where the hell is he? Smoke's voice keeps moving location. No matter what direction I face, I can find no trace of him.

"So you'd rather blame us for your inadequacies? No one stopped you from negotiating for your club. You don't deserve to head anything, let alone the organization my father founded. And stealing from us won't give you the deal with the Oliveris."

"Shut up! You and your sister never know when to quit." Silence follows Smoke's last outburst.

Lucien crouches and peers around the trailer on his side. His stance changes and he suddenly hurls himself at me. A gunshot disturbs the silence and Lucien's body hits mine with unimaginable force and a burning sensation tunnels through my chest. In the distance more weapons fire, but this time we aren't the target.

Lucien leans away from me and pain like I've never known radiates where Lucien's shoulder connected with my chest.

Shit!

"Getting shot hurts like a bitch," I say.

"I've been shot before, I'll survive this little nick." Lucien smiles at me. "It sounds like Mama Bear and your other reinforcements are here."

He doesn't know and I don't think I have much time to tell him. Not when there's something more important he deserves to know.

I touch his cheek. "Lucien, I need to tell you…"

"Can it wait until we get out of here, sweetheart?" He turns his attention to the shootout happening around us.

My hand travels to his mouth. His lips have been at once infuriating and a blessing with his sweet and dirty talk and the best kisses I've ever received. My vision begins to darken. I have to say this before it's too late. "I'm sorry it took me so long to say this…but I love you so much."

His startled gaze returns to me and the blood blooming on my chest. Blood that doesn't originate from his wound.

"Nooo!" Lucien's anguished scream is the last sound I hear before everything goes black.

CHAPTER SIXTEEN

Lucien

*H*ow am I just now realizing the blood on Zaïre's shirt isn't from my wound when I fell against her? Hurriedly, I press against her chest trying my damndest to stop the flow. It's the last surviving instinct from my field training to kick in. Everything else I do is based on emotion.

I've probably lost the men I had watching our backs. Grief hammers me while I try to save the one person I need to survive. I don't know what will happen after this, how I'll cope with the loss of my men, but if I can't save Zaïre, there will be no recovering from the emptiness she'll leave behind.

"Stay with me, sweetheart. This ain't how we end. Do you hear me? You're walking out of here alive!" My vision blurs and wetness seeps onto my cheek. Zaïre's last words were supposed to be a gift, not a fucking farewell.

The gunfight surrounding us fades to nothing, and the world reduces to Zaïre and me. I crush her against my body, her faded complexion doing nothing to ease the pain in my heart. "You aren't supposed to tell me you love me until you were ready to get married."

Shouts behind me try to pull me away from Zaïre but I bury my face in her shoulder, whispering and demanding for her to stay alive no matter what. Pain explodes behind my head and I black out.

When I open my eyes, a throbbing pain in my head makes everything fuzzy. It takes me a couple seconds before the room I'm in becomes clear, and the pain reduces to a low thrum. I'm in a hospital room, and a male nurse stitches the wound in my shoulder.

"Oh, you're awake. Lie still. I've applied a local anesthetic, but if you move around too much, you'll cause scarring."

My last vision of a bloody Zaïre comes flooding back to me and I disobey the nurse's order. I attempt to rise, but I'm strapped into the bed tight. "Where's Zaïre? Zaïre! I have to see her."

"Hold on, big guy. If you're talking about the woman who came in with you, she's in surgery. She was in pretty bad shape and lost a lot of blood. The EMTs couldn't get you to calm down in the ambulance when you woke up the first time and had to sedate you. If you keep acting up, we'll sedate you again."

My mind races. "What about her sisters? Are any of them here? Jojo, Thalie, or Camille? What about her father, Hammer? I mean Émile."

While I continue to negotiate to see someone who might know more about Zaïre's condition, my brother enters the room.

"Darren, thank fuck! Tell me what's happening."

Regret fills his eyes. "The bullet that shot you lodged inside Zaïre. It nicked an artery…they don't know what her chances are yet." His words sucker punch my solar plexus, making it difficult for me to breathe.

I shake my head in denial while gasping for breath. "No, that's bullshit. Zaïre is strong. She'll get through this. She has to. Because if she doesn't—"

"Then don't think about that. Concentrate on what you'll do when she recovers. In the meantime, pull yourself together. Mom and Dad will be here soon."

The nurse applies the final stitches on my shoulder. "We can probably arrange for you to be in the same recovery room."

"I'll make the arrangements," Darren says. He turns to leave.

"Wait. I can't be alone right now. I'll go mad without knowing about Zaïre. Tell me what I've missed. Who did we lose?"

My brother's shoulder stiffens.

I look to the nurse. "Can you give us the room?"

She hesitates, then nods. "I or a doctor will be by to give you more details about your injury."

Darren waits until she leaves to face me. "The sisters, Blake and Carter are safe. The Connollys' crew and Mama Bear's team have minor injuries. We had to medevac our men to other trauma hospitals. If we're lucky, they'll make it, but we don't have any news on their status yet."

"What of the police?"

"Our cover story is you saved Zaïre from a stalker."

"And they believe that?"

"With the Connollys backing us up, they have little choice."

"And what happened with that piece of shit cocksucker?"

Darren closes the door to my room alerting me I'm not going to like whatever he's about to say. "You need to stay calm for this."

"Out with it Darren. Today is not the day."

"We got his men, but Smoke got away during the shootout."

"Call a conference. I want every available agent on the call. We're going after him. I won't rest until I put him in the ground."

"I'm handling Smoke from here on out. You have to recover and take care of your woman. With the severity of her injury, it'll take time before she can go toe to toe with you again." Darren's stance dares me to argue with him.

"Using Zaïre is a low blow, even for you."

"He made Camille cry."

"He fucking shot my future wife."

"Who'll be my future sister-in-law. You can fight it all you want. I'm still going to be the last person he sees when he takes his last breath. In the meantime, you make sure Zaïre exchanges those vows."

"This argument ain't over."

We exchange steely stares. I fold first. With me strapped to a hospital bed I won't be winning any arguments with my brother. Not when he has so much to prove to Camille. Unlike Zaïre who knows her ass belongs by my side for the rest of our lives.

"I'd call you a son of a bitch if it didn't mean insulting my mother," I say.

"There are a few names I refrain from calling you daily. Goes with the brotherly territory."

Émile burst through the door looking years older than his age. "They said you'd got yourself injured. Imma tell you now, that wound in your shoulder is the only thing saving your ass, you heard me. The doctor said you throwing your-self in front of Zaïre saved her life."

"Is she out of surgery?" I ask.

"Just about. They're closing her up as we speak."

I send Darren a speaking glance and he leaves. He'll make sure she's by my side when she wakes up.

"How're you going to make sure that this shit with Smoke doesn't escalate into a war?" I glare at Émile. "Keep in mind if you'd been more transparent with your suspicions, we could have avoided this entire mess."

"I was in a difficult position then. Now, I have reason to take my club back and force out Smoke's supporters. There will be no war between my Hellraisers and Zaïre's Flossers."

"Don't blame me if I doubt your abilities, and be assured I will take down anyone who gets in my way."

❧❧❧❧

As soon as the nursing staff releases me from the straps on my bed, I sit my ass in the chair next to Zaïre. The cold material against my bare ass warms quickly. I'm still in the hospital gown because I'm running Darren ragged with all my demands and he has yet to return with a fresh set of clothes. The ones I arrived in have my and Zaïre's blood all over them. I'll have Darren burn them. I don't need the memory of how close I came to losing her as a constant reminder. What I long for now is for Zaïre to open her eyes.

She woke up from her anesthesia once but fell asleep from the residual effects. I'm lucky to have this time alone with her as her family is bound to monopolize her, and I'm not ready for that yet. I want to grab her and hold her close, but I tame the selfish impulse and rest my head on her thigh and hold her hand in mine.

For countless hours I sit this way, absorbing every breath she takes. At some point, I fall asleep but a hand brushing my hair back wakes me immediately. Zaïre's eyes are slits and a small smile plays at the edges of her mouth.

"How do you feel?" I ask.

"Water," she rasps.

"I can give you ice, but no water yet." I spoon out ice chips, worrying over her like a mother hen.

As if the staff has some psychic ability, a female nurse enters. "Good, you're up. We need to get you walking. It will help speed your recovery." She does some hocus pocus to the wires and machines and ushers Zaïre down the hall with me at their heels.

I refuse to let my siren out of my sight. I'm there next to her for the entire walk down the wing and on her return. When I've convinced myself that she won't fall the short distance to the bed without me waiting to catch her, I rush there first and wait to situate her. Time stretches and we don't speak. Me because there are so many words stuck in my throat that all want to come out at once. She because her eyes are drooping again.

The next morning the rest of her family arrives, but I refuse to move from my seated position next to Zaïre while they fawn over her. I quell the small resentment because I don't have a monopoly on my siren, no matter how much I want to shut us away from the world, and I know how important her family is.

When the Roudanez family leaves, Zaïre turns to me, her eyes clearer than they were yesterday. "I can tell you have something you're holding back from me." Her words release the levies holding everything inside me.

"Don't you dare act so glib after what you did to me. I swear if you'd died… I would go to hell and force the devil to return your soul."

"You think I'm going to hell?"

"With the lives we lead, we'll need a miracle to get us into heaven. But even in hell, you won't be able to escape me."

She smiles, a small muscle movement nothing like the ones she's given me before, but it starts my heart pumping harder because I know there will be more days and more smiles to come. "Shouldn't you be afraid of the devil? I hear he's pretty possessive."

"You think the devil frightens me? The only thing that does is having to spend a lifetime without you."

Her mouth turns down in a frown warning me she's ready for a fight. "So you throw yourself in front of a bullet that could have killed you, too? That is such a pussy move. And don't even come at me with that whole, 'I'm your man. It's what I do' bullshit. Because all that means is you can't handle me dying, so you'll die instead and leave me to suffer without you for the rest of my life. And you say you want to marry me."

"You know that's not how it is."

She slaps my hand away and grumbles, "You could have told me to duck."

"Because you're faster than a bullet?"

"Despite your argument—"

"My valid argument."

"—and Smoke's failed attack, I'm here. I said I loved you—"

"And then you tried to die on me."

"So, what you going to do now? Bitch at me until I do die?"

"Sweetheart, I've told you about that mouth of yours." I stand and walk towards the door.

"Where you going?"

"I'm making sure I hear the words I want coming from your sweet lips." I leave without another word, uncaring who gets a flash of my ass, only to return dragging the Chaplain and a random nurse I found behind me.

"Lord Jesus. What are you doing?" Zaïre raises her bed until she's sitting straight.

I bypass her to go to the folder of documents Darren

dropped off earlier after completing one of the many tasks I gave him before leaving to fulfill another. Without explaining, I shove the folder into the Chaplain's hands. No one is going to delay me from my goals any further. Nor can anyone question my priorities.

"Let's get this started." I resume my spot beside Zaïre.

"I have to make sure she consents," the Chaplain says.

Her eyes widen in understanding. "Is this even legal?" she asks.

"Do you think for one second I'd give you room to wiggle out of this?"

"She consents! She consents!" Zaïre grasps my hand.

My siren frantically fans her eyes with her free hand. I've seen my mother do the same thing when she gets overly emotional. Like with my mother, the action doesn't dispel the sheen in Zaïre's eyes.

"How…when did you arrange this?"

"My brother and parents are very motivated to make you an official member of the Connors family. Everything the state of Texas needs to declare you legally mine is here in this room." I hand her the ring she will place on my finger, eager to do the same to hers.

In no time I hear the "I do" I've been dreaming of since the first night we spent together leave Zaïre's lips. Before the Chaplain can finish declaring us man and wife I lower my mouth to devour Zaïre's. By the time I come up for air, we're alone once more.

"Now Mrs. Connors, you'll have to follow your doctor's instructions and get better soon so I can start rewarding my good girl for the rest of our lives."

EPILOGUE

Zaïre

*T*oday marks three months since my first wedding. I stand in my second wedding dress in the reception hall watching my guests in what is technically my third wedding.

Lucien's mother, the classy Mrs. Lorraine Connors, nearly started a drag-out, down-and-dirty brawl with my mama over what they considered my official wedding. Since nothing was going to beat the hospital wedding with its lack of fanfare, I told them to plan two, and Lucien and I would show up and play our part. That of course, started another competition between Maxine and Lorraine to see who could out-wedding the other.

Lorraine's wedding was on a ranch with cowboys and my husband took too much delight in "roping himself a bride." Despite the brief rodeo element, it was a classy affair. The mayor of Bourbon attended to wish us well.

Mama's wedding incorporated some of the New Orleans traditions, like dance krewes and street vendors. But I'm most excited about what we're lining up for now. A good old wedding second line. I search the sea of heads for the blond that stole my heart and who'll be following the brass band out of the reception hall.

Pær Guillaume has his arm around Ms. Bertie and is whispering something in her ear to cause her to giggle like a schoolgirl. Daddy's got Mama up against the wall, half-hidden from the gaggle of people, but they ain't fooling nobody. Daddy's getting his sugar in before the music starts. Meanwhile, Lorraine and Ethan listen avidly to Jojo as she points to the band and demonstrates a few of her favorite moves.

As has been happening almost daily, my heart gives a joyful jump when I catch sight of Lucien. His dimples are on full display and his wide smile is evidence he's just as happy as I am.

Although everything from three months ago hasn't been resolved, there's been progress. Daddy successfully won his old position back. Smoke's betrayal and bad decisions hit Daddy pretty hard. He's been cleaning up messes and putting out fires since his club reinstated him as their president. One positive that came from the situation is he no longer talks about the Flossers as his daughters' little hobby.

Lucien lost a man on his team. He grieves for him in the quiet moments at home, but not to the point where he numbs the pain with alcohol. Instead, we're creating a foundation to benefit the families of employees he loses in the field. The work seems to help focus his energies. If Lucien isn't busy getting the foundation up and running, he's hands-deep in relocating his corporate office. Texas will still be a hub, but Lucien and the men willing to move will call New Orleans home.

I join Lucien behind the band, Go-cup in hand, and we start our parade. Our route will go all the way to the French Quarter, which is a little more than I need, but no less fun.

"Sweetheart, you know what day today is, don't you?" Lucien leans down to my ear so only I hear him.

I roll my eyes. Of course, he is referring to my appointment this morning. My doctor declared I can resume all my prior activities, but Lucien is only interested in one kind.

"I have a lot of time to make up for with my poor, neglected pussy," he says.

My body immediately responds. Abstinence only makes it worse. I have three months of pent-up desire to let loose and my husband's reminder only makes me want this reception to be over yesterday.

"It's your own fault. I was willing to be creative. My mouth wasn't under doctor's orders—"

"Sweetheart, you and I know you ain't ever satisfied with just a taste. And no orgasm is worth causing a grimace of pain to cross your pretty lips." Lucien emphasizes his point with a lingering kiss. "Now, frustration from the many ways I'll withhold your orgasm tonight is another story. Your face when you finally come will more than make up for these last three months."

"Hmph, get in line. Since I've been a good girl by following all the doctor's orders, it's only right I get to decide my first reward of the night. And you know what my favorite reward is." I lick my lips and wink at him.

"Fuck, sweetheart. You're only going to make my pussy suffer when I fuck you until you can't walk."

"You can try." I attempt to walk away from him, but he grabs my hand and pulls me into him for a searing kiss.

The crowd surrounds us, but I'm only aware of Lucien's lips and tongue devouring me. I will never tire of his mouth.

A hand on my shoulder pulls us apart and it takes me a few seconds to understand what I'm seeing.

A disheveled Darren holds Lucien by his lapels, his panic-filled eyes forewarning me. I'm not going to like what he has to say.

"He fucking took her, Lucien. Smoke took Camille!"

SNEAK PEEK

Thank you so much for reading Ruthless Protector.

Please leave a review if you to let me know how you enjoyed Lucien and Zaïre's story.

Continue reading to discover your next book boyfriend in my new novel **Maid for the Yakuza**.

MAID FOR THE YAKUZA

CHAPTER ONE

*T*he little kitten has no idea the danger she's courting. She is my business partner's new sister-in-law. That alone should have stopped the images in my head every time she turned those curious brown eyes on me. But she can't hide her underlying attraction. Not when her lips part and I glimpse her eager tongue licking her full mouth. Nor when she stands still while the well wishers blur around her.

No, that is my interest in her. I've honed in on her and her guileless reaction to me, awakening the dormant dragon inside. I would love to blame everything on the outpouring of love from the newlyweds and the romantically decorated yard, but they didn't move me when I first spied them. They don't affect me now.

This is madness. I prefer my women bold, strong, and with a fire that drives them to take what they want. As beautiful as this woman is with her warm, brown complexion, she's too timid for my liking.

So, why are my eyes drawn to her wherever she moves?

"Oyassan." My younger cousin, Takeshi, who is also my

wakagashira approaches from behind me. "Tread carefully with that one. Our alliance is still shaky with the Oliveris. Problems with him could impact our more legitimate businesses."

I glance behind me.

"You're right. Whatever you decide about her, I will take care of any issues that arise."

Words are not always necessary to convey my thoughts to Takeshi due to our many years growing up together as siblings. That's why we work well together now. He can translate any look I send his way.

Although I divert my attention to the newlyweds on the dance floor, Takeshi's focus remains on the woman. He sighs. "I know where this is going, even if you won't acknowledge it. I only ask that you think about the consequences to me. If you give Shinji reason to complain, you won't get any peace either."

I refrain from rolling my eyes. As threats go, Shinji is an effective one. I hate watching him pout because I'm over-working his lover. It's moot at this point. I don't intend to make a move, no matter how tempting the package may be.

Takeshi shrugs. My silence drives him to rejoin Shinji where they network with some of the more prominent wedding guests. Neither strays too far, as they like to keep me in sight for my safety.

Laughable, really. My grandfather trained me well. It's not conceit when I say I'm the most dangerous person in the room.

A new song plays, one meant for lovers, and I fight with myself not to claim her. I have no business approaching her. My fight proves needless because when I succumb to her allure and turn for another glimpse, I only have to look down. Portia Waters stands before me, a woman with an inexplicable pull. I frown, hating my inability to control my body's reaction to her.

Her expressive eyes widen in panic, although the emotion is quickly wiped from her face. But she can't hide the underlying pain dulling what should be a rich velvety hue. Someone taught her to hide herself. To stand in front of a threat and brace herself instead of listening to her instincts and fleeing for protection, or fighting for her right to exist. As if the consequences bore deep beneath her skin to her soul. But the glimpse of a tiger's strength peeks through.

Maybe there's more to her after all.

She straightens her shoulders and breathes an almost inaudible breath. "Dance with me." With a tilt to her chin, she holds my stare.

It's a prey's dare. A sign no predator can resist. And that's what I am, what I've been reared to be. I take her onto the dance floor and pull her close. It takes everything to control my body's instant reaction to her softness, to her fresh understated scent. Her body cushions me, overflowing my hands. I grip her tighter, pressing her to my chest until there is no distinguishing her black dress from my tuxedo.

The silken bun on her head tickles my cheek making my fingers itch to pull it down and bask in her glorious mane. Although the tight style reveals no hint of its length, I sense when she looses the strands it will be marvelous. Her head rests on my shoulder, a weight that feels fated. Despite the sharp angle, all I see is her. Our bodies move in sync, the lyrics from the Lauryn Hill rendition of "I Can't Take My Eyes Off You" too close to the truth for me to start a conversation.

"Thank you for not rejecting me," she says.

Her word choice strikes me as odd. An underlying vulnerability hints at many rejections far more serious than a dance. Unreasonable anger fills me. Anger for the faceless people who made my sometimes kitten sometimes tigress feel unworthy.

What the hell is happening to me?

"Don't put more stock in my accepting your request than you should. I'd be a fool to reject a beautiful woman," I say, surprising myself. If not for my close hold on her, we would tumble to the ground when Portia stumbles from my unplanned response. Less surprising is the absence of emotion in my voice, a habit drilled into me from a young age to leave people guessing that has become second nature to me.

At least I didn't destroy what little of my self-respect I hold by demanding to know who I need to kill for making her feel undeserving. There's no reason to show these Oliveris the fruits of my semi-civilized upbringing.

My restraint breaks before we complete two turns on the dance floor. "Who rejected you?"

"Hm? Just people." Portia burrows closer as if trying to find an opening where she can rest beneath my skin.

I don't hate it and that's a problem. Although I have more money than most can spend in twenty lifetimes, I'm certain I can't afford to want her this much. But logic has lost its usual stranglehold on my mouth. "What did these people do?"

She shrugs. "We're at a wedding. Let's only discuss happy things to celebrate the occasion."

I reign in my impatience. It's too late to pretend that she doesn't affect me. That I won't obsess over this puzzle until I know everything. That I won't obsess over her until I discover all her secrets. Everything she thinks to hide from me, I will uncover.

"Tell me this, how did your sister meet Gio? You two are different from everyone else in his circle."

The closing notes to the song we're dancing to fade, but I

keep leading her into the next selection. She doesn't seem to notice.

"The honest truth is I don't know. I was surprised to get the invitation since Jessie and I haven't spoken to each other in years. But everything was so fancy from the personal delivery to the invitation package. I had to see what it all meant." Portia's voice holds a wealth of regret that pulls at me although I don't deal in regrets.

Regrets are for the weak. Life as I've known it has tried to kill me since as far back as I can remember, forging my strength into the strongest element on earth. The sophisticated veneer I display to the public hides my lethality. I have no time for regrets or weakness. Despite all that, I find myself making time for future regrets with the woman in my arms.

Is there nothing I can do to resist her?

Portia raises her head and pierces me with her large, cognac eyes. "Sleep with me tonight."

I stumble over my feet, not expecting her to speak, let alone say something so out of character with my assumptions.

"Is that what you truly want?" I ask. "Because if so, my answer is no." I pull away, intending to lead her off the floor, give my respects to the hosts and leave. I must put a stop to this unfathomable attraction. I no longer care that the overly amorous wedded couple haven't left their reception. Portia tempts me in a way I shouldn't be, and if we are in a room with a bed, sleep is the last thing either of us will do.

The sooner I get on the plane to California, the better.

She pulls on my sleeve. "Wait...I...uh..."

I wait, not really understanding why, but wanting to know what she'll say next.

An internal debate takes place behind her expressive eyes, displaying her doubts and fears, and the moment she decides to discard it all. "Let me follow you to your hotel where I'll fuck you until you've forgotten your name."

What man can deny that invitation?

Yes! Jessie's sister, Portia from Inevitable finally gets a story. Find out what happens when Katsuo accepts her invitation by getting your copy today.
https://www.amazon.com/dp/B0CCXFJJVJ

OTHER TITLES BY MELVERNA MCFARLANE

Jessie & Giorgio: Inescapable (Oliveri Mafia Book One)

René & Nico: Inevitable (Oliveri Mafia Book Two)

Onika & Lorenzo: Indomitable (Oliveri Mafia Book Three)

Fayth & Keoni: A Test of Fayth: A Single Dad Romance (Heart of a Wounded Hero)

Celia & Everett: Everett: A Sweet and Steamy Café L'amour Duet

Sloane, Valentino & Tácito: Valentino DeLuca: Savage Bloodline

Yomaris & Lochlann: Caught Red Handed

Kenya & Cameron: Snaring Her Man

Aniyah & Aris: Vows & Vendettas

Portia & Katsuo: Maid for the Yakuza

Cantrelle & An Bao: Ruthless Enforcer (newsletter exclusive)

ABOUT THE AUTHOR

Melverna McFarlane loves love stories with Happily Ever Afters. After years of characters taunting her imagination with their potential, she decided it was time to write her own scorching hot romances. She moved to America from Jamaica at a young age, and has lived up and down the east coast most of her life. The bitterly cold winter of 2013 was the last straw, driving her back to island life—this time to Hawaii. When not writing, she is reading romance, YA, and Fantasy, country hopping, or vicariously obsessing over other people's cats, because she can't have one. She loves to hear from readers.

Join her on:

Patreon - https://www.patreon.com/MelvernaMcFarlane

Twitter - https://www.twitter.com/MelvernaM

Instagram - https://www.instagram.com/melverna_mcfarlane/

Facebook - https://www.facebook.com/melverna.mcfarlane

Website - www.MelvernaMcFarlane.com

Drop her a line, or tease her with pics and stories of your cat's antics. She might feature them in her next book.